AN OLD FRIEND

The Rangers raced past on the road.

"Too bad I can't claim the reward," said Slocum.

"Too bad you mighta cost me a pair of good men," came a cold voice. "Like you already cost me the services of Rufus Toombs."

Slocum swung around. He had not heard the man with the shotgun approach. He stared down the double barrels of that deadly weapon and knew the man holding it would squeeze the triggers and never think twice.

Slocum knew him all too well.

"Howdy, Jack," Slocum said. "It's been a spell."

"That it has, Slocum," answered Rebel Jack Holtz as he raised the weapon and sighted along the barrels. "And it's gonna be a lot longer till next time. See you in hell, Slocum."

DON'T MISS THESE
ALL-ACTION WESTERN SERIES
FROM THE BERKLEY PUBLISHING GROUP

THE GUNSMITH by J. R. Roberts

Clint Adams was a legend among lawmen, outlaws, and ladies. They called him . . . the Gunsmith.

LONGARM by Tabor Evans

The popular long-running series about Deputy U.S. Marshal Custis Long—his life, his loves, his fight for justice.

SLOCUM by Jake Logan

Today's longest-running action Western. John Slocum rides a deadly trail of hot blood and cold steel.

BUSHWHACKERS by B. J. Lanagan

An action-packed series by the creators of Longarm! The rousing adventures of the most brutal gang of cutthroats ever assembled—Quantrill's Raiders.

DIAMONDBACK by Guy Brewer

Dex Yancey is Diamondback, a Southern gentleman turned con man when his brother cheats him out of the family fortune. Ladies love him. Gamblers hate him. But nobody pulls one over on Dex . . .

WILDGUN by Jack Hanson

The blazing adventures of mountain man Will Barlow—from the creators of Longarm!

TEXAS TRACKER by Tom Calhoun

J. T. Law: the most relentless—and dangerous—manhunter in all Texas. Where sheriffs and posses fail, he's the best man to bring in the most vicious outlaws—for a price.

JAKE LOGAN

SLOCUM
AND THE
REBEL CANNON

J
JOVE BOOKS, NEW YORK

THE BERKLEY PUBLISHING GROUP
Published by the Penguin Group
Penguin Group (USA) Inc.
375 Hudson Street, New York, New York 10014, USA
Penguin Group (Canada), 90 Eglinton Avenue East, Suite 700, Toronto, Ontario M4P 2Y3, Canada
(a division of Pearson Penguin Canada Inc.)
Penguin Books Ltd., 80 Strand, London WC2R 0RL, England
Penguin Group Ireland, 25 St. Stephen's Green, Dublin 2, Ireland (a division of Penguin Books Ltd.)
Penguin Group (Australia), 250 Camberwell Road, Camberwell, Victoria 3124, Australia
(a division of Pearson Australia Group Pty. Ltd.)
Penguin Books India Pvt. Ltd., 11 Community Centre, Panchsheel Park, New Delhi—110 017, India
Penguin Group (NZ), 67 Apollo Drive, Rosedale, North Shore 0632, New Zealand
(a division of Pearson New Zealand Ltd.)
Penguin Books (South Africa) (Pty.) Ltd., 24 Sturdee Avenue, Rosebank, Johannesburg 2196,
South Africa

Penguin Books Ltd., Registered Offices: 80 Strand, London WC2R 0RL, England

This is a work of fiction. Names, characters, places, and incidents either are the product of the author's imagination or are used fictitiously, and any resemblance to actual persons, living or dead, business establishments, events, or locales is entirely coincidental.

SLOCUM AND THE REBEL CANNON

A Jove Book / published by arrangement with the author

PRINTING HISTORY
Jove edition / July 2008

Copyright © 2008 by The Berkley Publishing Group.
Cover illustration by Sergio Giovine.

ISBN: 978-0-515-14481-9

JOVE®
Jove Books are published by The Berkley Publishing Group,
a division of Penguin Group (USA) Inc.
375 Hudson Street, New York, New York 10014.
JOVE is a registered trademark of Penguin Group (USA) Inc.
The "J" design is a trademark belonging to Penguin Group (USA) Inc.

PRINTED IN THE UNITED STATES OF AMERICA

10 9 8 7 6 5 4 3 2 1

1

Some days, a man's luck ran dry. Other days, it was a torrent and he needed a slicker to keep from getting soaked. John Slocum drew rein, pushed back his battered black Stetson, and stared at the iron box sitting all bright and shiny on the bank of the arroyo. He had ridden due west most of the day after having crossed the Pecos near Red Bluff Lake. The hot Texas sun had beaten down on him mercilessly, but he had kept riding, wanting to reach El Paso in a couple days. He had no place to go and nothing to keep him where he was. It had been like that for the better part of a month after he had been fired at the Double Cross Ranch just north of Fort Worth. The ranch owner had gone bankrupt and gotten rid of most all his cowboys, Slocum included. There hadn't been any ill feelings. Slocum knew what it was like not having two nickels to rub together, and Xavier X. Benton had had a run of bad luck. Texas fever had ravaged his herd for most of a month; then lightning had struck a steer and stampeded the rest of the cattle.

By the time they had finished rounding up the beeves that had not been killed outright or run themselves to death, Benton had only one cow for every five that he had begun with that season. Slocum counted himself lucky in getting twenty dollars pay. He doubted the handful of cowboys sticking with Benton would end up with that much. Bad luck, sort of good luck. Slocum had taken his money and ridden away without so much as a glance back.

Pulling his bandanna from around his neck, he wiped sweat off his forehead, then carefully tied the bandanna again before standing in the stirrups and looking around. He was alone on the stretch of desert running all the way to the looming Guadalupe Mountains a day's travel ahead.

Slocum dismounted. His mare nickered in gratitude, and shifted about without a rider's weight for the first time in hours. He patted the horse's neck, then dropped the reins and went to the strongbox. Staring at it a moment, he wondered what the chances were of finding anything in it.

"Slim, none," Slocum said, pushing his Stetson even higher on his forehead. Still, his luck hadn't been all bad lately. He knelt and swung the box around. A sturdy lock held the hasp shut. Grabbing a nearby rock, Slocum hammered away at the lock for a minute or two before it gave up and broke with a loud snap. He jerked away the lock and tossed it aside.

Not sure what to expect, he opened the lid slowly. A smile spread across his face, like the first rays of dawn lighting up an entire day with sunlight. Slocum pulled out a thick sheaf of greenbacks and leafed through them.

"I spent two months punching cattle for Benton and got twenty dollars. By keeping an eye on the trail, I just made myself at least five hundred dollars." Laughing, he stood, kicked the box away, and put the wad of scrip into his saddlebags. It might take him a couple months to spend this much money, even with a full bottle of whiskey a day. If he rode on into Mexico, chose tequila or pulque over rye whiskey, he could live like a king for six months.

The thought of a pretty señorita to go along with the tequila made spending the money even more alluring. He mounted and put his heels to his horse's flanks. El Paso beckoned. And maybe San Miguel de Allende down south in the heart of Mexico. Or one of the towns along the western coast of Mexico. The notion of sitting with that señorita, staring out over blue water and enjoying a cool breeze, provided him with incentive to keep riding in the heat of the day.

He was so lost in the warmth of the sun and the heat of his Mexican fantasies that he failed to see the two soldiers sitting under a mesquite bush near the road until he was almost upon them.

"Hold on, mister," called the one with corporal's stripes on his arm. The soldier levered himself to his feet using his rifle, which he hoisted to his shoulder so he could draw a bead on Slocum.

Slocum squinted at the two troopers.

"You from Fort Quitman?" he asked.

"We're the ones askin' the questions," snapped the private. He lifted his rifle and trained it on Slocum, too.

"Didn't hear any questions," Slocum pointed out. He wasn't unduly upset over the way the soldiers poked their rifle barrels in his direction. The Apaches in this part of West Texas were a constant problem, and the men who supplied them with rifles and ammunition were even more so. Since he obviously did not drive a wagon loaded with guns for illegal trade, he had nothing to worry about.

"You got a mouth on you, don't you?" The corporal drew back the hammer on his carbine and his finger turned white as he squeezed the trigger. This got Slocum's attention. He turned slightly in the saddle and inched his hand toward the hammer of his Colt Navy. He didn't have a ghost of a chance to draw and fire before the soldier pulled off his round, but he was not going down without a fight.

"My curse," Slocum said easily. He studied the men more carefully now and wondered why neither wore standard-issue cavalry boots. One wore plain boots, and the corporal had fancier hand-tooled ones, probably bought in Mexico. This didn't mean neither was a cavalry trooper since supply problems on the frontier were always a concern, but other things made Slocum wary of them.

"That curse'll put you in a grave," the private said. Slocum didn't glance in the man's direction. He locked eyes with the corporal. Slocum's green eyes made the man uneasy enough that the rifle wavered a mite. The muzzle dipped down, away from Slocum's torso.

"What can I do for you?" Slocum finally asked.

"Been a robbery. We're lookin' for the road agent responsible."

"Now what was it that got robbed? A stagecoach?"

"How'd you know that?"

"Found a strongbox a couple miles back," he said, jerking his thumb over his shoulder.

"Do tell." The corporal sighted in on Slocum again.

"If you'll point that carbine in another direction, I'll show you what I found inside it."

"You got the money?" The private almost dropped his rifle in his eagerness to go to Slocum's side.

"Found maybe five hundred dollars in greenbacks," Slocum said, wondering if he should have even mentioned finding the strongbox. He had little choice, though, since the soldiers had the drop on him and were likely to search him and his saddlebags eventually. Better to confess to finding the money than to let them come across it on their own.

"You look, Hez," the corporal said eagerly. "I got the varmint covered. Mister, I'll ventilate you if you so much as twitch."

"No need. I'm willing to turn it in. Is the stagecoach company offering a reward for finding it?"

"Ain't no reward," the private said, ripping off the rawhide string holding Slocum's saddlebags to his saddle. The man staggered away in his hurry to paw through the contents. He let out a whoop like an Apache warrior and held up a handful of money. "Lookee here what I got!"

"Reckon we got the money and the robber," the corporal said.

"Why would I tell you I had anything in my gear if I was the road agent responsible for stealing it? How long's it been anyway? I don't see stage tracks along the road. The way I figure it, the driver tossed the strongbox down while he was being chased by the road agents to keep it from being stolen."

Truth was, the soft sand filling the twin ruts of the road Slocum followed wouldn't hold tracks for more than a few hours. The restless hot wind would erase any trace. He hadn't even seen any hoofprints left by the two soldiers' horses.

" 'Cuz you're one sneaky son of a bitch," the private said. "That's why you'd tell us, to get us all het up so you could get the drop on us and kill us."

"Shut up, Hez," the corporal said without venom. He had endured all this rambling before and had tired of it.

Slocum heard the private reaching for his rifle and saw the way the corporal tensed up. They were going to gun him down. He let out a loud moan, threw up his left hand, and knocked off his hat, sending it sailing through the air behind him. Both men shifted their attention to the hat. This was enough for Slocum to slap leather and drag out his six-shooter from his holster.

He fired at the corporal and caught the soldier square in the center of the chest. The man grunted and simply sat down. He dumbly reached for the tiny red spot blossoming on his blue jacket. Slocum paid him no more attention, bending low, sawing at the reins, and getting his mare moving in a tight circle. The private was getting his wits back and fired a wild shot that ripped across Slocum's back. He felt a moment of hot pain and then nothing.

His attention focused entirely on the soldier who had been in the road behind him. Slocum snapped off another shot at the private, but missed. Then his horse reared, making another shot impossible.

By the time Slocum got his mare under control, the soldier had lit out for the cover of nearby sand dunes. Slocum got a shot off at the man as he disappeared over the rise.

"Whoa, calm down, good, good," Slocum soothed. The mare snorted and showed whites around big brown eyes. Slocum patted the horse on the neck and soothed her further. Then he had to make a decision. The private had lit out with the money from the strongbox. More than that, Slocum doubted any cavalry trooper would let his partner's death go unavenged. The corporal lay sprawled on his back. Flies already buzzed about the body, and a quick look into the clear blue sky showed hungry buzzards spiraling lower and lower.

If the two soldiers were part of a larger detachment, the sight of the vultures would bring the rest of the squad on the run. Slocum could ride off, leaving behind the private—and the cash—or he could tend to it. There wasn't any doubt in his mind that the two soldiers had intended to murder him for the money.

That made his ire rise. He slammed his Colt Navy back into its holster and drew the Winchester from its sheath. Levering in a round, he called out, "Give me the money and I'll ride on."

"Go to hell!"

Slocum turned a little in the saddle. The private had moved along behind a sand dune, going westward, paralleling the road.

"Come on, Hez. It's not worth you ending up like the corporal. You tried to dry-gulch me. Nobody's going to hold that against you," Slocum lied, "but I want the money."

"It's not yours!"

"Hez, come on. It's not yours either." Slocum listened hard for a reply. He wanted the soldier to keep talking so he could track his progress behind the dune. At the end, about twenty yards away, it sloped down into a saddle. If the private wanted to find safety behind the next dune over, he had to cross that depression.

Even as the idea hit Slocum, the soldier bolted from cover and ran as hard as he could. Slocum lifted his Winchester to his shoulder, let out a breath, and squeezed the trigger at the same time. The hard slam against his shoulder went unnoticed. He was too busy watching the private.

The man had gone down with Slocum's shot, but there wasn't the right *feel* to it. The shot had been good—but not a killing shot.

"Quit playing possum," Slocum called, dismounting and walking toward the fallen man. He got no response, but this only made him more alert. He kept his rifle trained on the soldier, and it saved his life.

When he got within a dozen feet, the private rolled over and fired a pistol he must have kept hidden under his shirt. His awkward position caused the shot to go wide. Slocum's return fire caught the soldier smack in the middle of the face.

Even knowing it was an instantly lethal shot, Slocum advanced cautiously and kicked the pistol from the soldier's hand. Only then did he roll him onto his back. He quickly found the wad of greenbacks and tucked them into his own shirt pocket. Slocum patted the big lump and backed away.

High above, he heard the raucous calls from a dozen or more buzzards. Not ten feet away, a coyote watched him with hot yellow eyes. Slocum walked faster. The coyote rushed to his meal.

Slocum returned to his skittish horse. He gentled the horse again, mounted, and rode away from the four buzzards already pulling at the corporal's flesh. Glad to leave the massacre behind him, Slocum kept his horse at a trot for longer than he ought to in such heat, but the mare was willing. The smell of fresh blood had caused her nostrils to flare.

"Not a very hospitable place," Slocum said, looking around the barren landscape. It had not changed in the past hour, but his appraisal of it had. Finding the money had been a stroke of good luck, but the two murderous cavalry troopers had turned the luck against him again. To reassure himself, Slocum patted the wad of scrip in his pocket. He had sweated so much, the once-thick bundle had flattened and even molded itself to the shape of his body.

His horse began to flag, so Slocum hunted for a watering hole. The Guadalupe Mountains were not one inch closer, or so it seemed. Distances in the desert were always deceptive. But the terrain had changed a little, going from hard desert to one spotted with greasewood and ocotillo to go along with the mesquite. Occasional patches of prickly pear cactus told him there must be some water nearby. They could seemingly grow on solid rock, but their roots did not go down to the center of the earth like those of the mesquite. He had heard that five hundred feet of mesquite root had been pulled up by some enterprising rancher farther south. To keep the thorny bush from taking over the prairies, the Comanche had burned them off every year. Even this had not killed the hardy plants, only kept them down so grasses fit for grazing horses could grow.

Slocum released his tight grip on the reins and gave the mare her head when she began getting restive. Although he had not spotted it, the horse had scented a watering hole. They left the road and meandered around dunes and into a rocky patch. He saw cottonwood trees growing, and knew he had found his oasis in the middle of this desolate land.

Knowing dangerous animals had to water here, too, Slocum approached cautiously. He saw tracks of coyotes, rabbits, and even a lone deer in the mud circling the pond. The fact that there were only a few piles of bleached bones told him the water was probably sweet and cool. If there had been a large number of skeletons, the water would have been responsible. As it was, a handful of incautious beasts had been killed by quicker, hungrier predators.

Just to be sure, Slocum scooped up a single cupped hand of water and sniffed it before tasting the glorious wetness. No bitter alkali taste.

"Don't drink too much," Slocum warned his horse, letting the mare thrust her nose down to the water.

"Could give you the same advice," came a cold voice.

Slocum reached for his six-shooter, but froze when he heard the metallic click of a cocking rifle. "Who might you be?"

"Now, you got things all ass backward," came the answer. "I ask, you answer. You know anything about gunfire 'bout an hour back? I saw buzzards high up in the sky earlier in the day, but not now."

"Sun can do bad things to a man's eyes," Slocum said. He looked down into the pool and caught the reflection of the man in the limbs of the cottonwood behind him. While the image was indistinct, he saw that the rifle trained on his back did not waver. It seemed to Slocum that he had had his fill of having men prodding him with questions and pointing rifles at him.

"Not to mine," the man said. "I was whelped by a sidewinder and raised by a coyote."

The ripples in the water momentarily obscured the reflection, but Slocum caught enough to see that the man was climbing down out of the cottonwood tree. To do this he had to lift the muzzle of his rifle.

Moving fast, Slocum dropped, rolled, and went for his six-gun. He had it out and pointed in the direction of the tree, only to find the rifleman was hidden by the thick trunk.

"You give up and drop that gun. I'm a Texas Ranger and you're under arrest!"

"What for?" Slocum froze. His finger was halfway back on the trigger. It didn't make no never-mind to him if he killed a road agent or a Ranger. Anyone who pointed a gun in his direction deserved the same fate.

"You're a feisty one," the Ranger said, keeping the tree between him and Slocum.

Exposed by the edge of the pool, Slocum knew he had to get to cover before the Texas Ranger found himself a spot where he could hide and shoot at the same time.

Slocum rolled left and then flung himself hard to the right and kept rolling. A tiny puff of dirt popped up where he had been, showing how near the bullet had come to killing him. Slocum got to his feet, feinted, and then found himself some cover behind a fallen log. It was half-rotted and a rifle slug would rip right on through it, but Slocum wanted it more to hide than for protection. He took a few seconds to get his wits about him and figure out what had to be done.

"You're only makin' it worse on yourself," the Ranger called. Slocum followed the sound of the voice. The man was retreating from the tree, going through some underbrush. The faint sound of a horse whinnying told Slocum the Texas Ranger wanted to get mounted.

Slocum could retreat himself, but then he would have a Ranger on his tail, on top of everyone else already looking for him. Reloading, Slocum gathered his feet under him and then exploded up and out, running hard for the cottonwood where the Ranger had laid his ambush. Using the same tree for cover, Slocum spotted the lawman and fired twice.

"Damn you, I'll see you swing for this," the Ranger cried. "You shot me!"

Slocum didn't bother to answer. If he had hit his foe, it had been little more than a scratch. The Ranger was trying to lure him closer.

Crouching down, aiming his six-shooter, Slocum waited. During the war he had been a sniper, and a good one. He might sit for hours in a tree waiting for the flash of sunlight off a Yankee officer's gold braid. A single expert shot could turn the tide of battle, and often had. Slocum had developed patience enough to make the ones he hunted antsy. For more than ten minutes, he held his position, breathing shallowly and keeping his eyes moving for any sign of the Ranger.

Slocum had to hand it to the lawman. He had patience, too, but eventually he came to think that Slocum had slipped away. Foolishly, he stood up to look around. Slocum was ready when he did. His finger drew back the rest of the way on his six-shooter and sent a slug flying.

The Texas Ranger grunted and fell back into the thicket. Slocum waited another minute, but the lawman did not move a muscle.

It was prudent to put another slug into the Ranger's body to be sure, but Slocum chose to slip back and find his mare. He mounted and rode steadily westward toward the Guadalupe Mountains. Finding the money had been a godsend for him, but his luck had turned bad after that. He had killed two soldiers and maybe a Ranger. No matter it had been in self-defense both times. Slocum knew Texas was suddenly no place to linger.

It was time to see what Arizona or even California had to offer in the way of sanctuary.

2

John Slocum rode into the dusty, dry town of Sidewinder looking all around. He had reached the foothills and had spotted a road leading deeper into the Guadalupe Mountains. Thinking it might afford more in the way of water than continuing along the road heading for El Paso, and with his horse badly in need of rest, he had followed the winding canyons until he came onto this little town sitting in the saddle between two sheer cliffs. The residents must not have any fear of rock slides since they lived smack between a pair of hundred-foot-tall mesas. It made Slocum a mite uneasy, but he rode ahead past the town's crudely lettered sign and down the main street, such as it was.

He had seen a hundred other towns that looked identical. There was no good reason for Sidewinder to exist, yet it did. The ground was too rocky for crops, there didn't seem to be any mining going on in the surrounding hills, and yet the town was here. All Slocum could figure was that this road led somewhere north and was the shortest way there.

"From nowhere to nowhere," he grumbled under his breath. All he wanted was to be on his way as quickly as possible. Two dead soldiers, and a Texas Ranger either dead or so close to it that it didn't matter, lay behind him.

When they were discovered, he might have not only the entire Ninth and Tenth Cavalry after him, but also a passel of Texas Rangers.

He drew his mare to a dead halt in the center of the street, and simply stared at a sign swinging slowly in the feeble breeze. Slocum would have spat but his mouth was too dry.

The sign read: RANGER COMPANY G. The building looked deserted, but Slocum knew better than to poke his nose inside to find out. He had found the town where an entire company of Texas Rangers called their home. It was definitely time to keep moving. If the Ranger he had plugged lived and got word to any of his partners, it would end up here in Sidewinder, maybe in this very building.

Slocum snapped his reins and got the tired mare moving farther along the main street to a solitary saloon. It was late afternoon, and folks had yet to quit their jobs and come pouring in to swap lies and knock back bitter, warm beer. This was about perfect for Slocum. He could wet his whistle, have his horse tended to, and be a mile down the trail before anyone noticed.

He rode farther down the street to the livery and dismounted. It took the better part of ten minutes' haggling to pay over the two dollars for his horse to be fed and groomed.

"That there mare's hobblin' a mite," the stable man said. "You notice that? Front right hoof."

"Do tell." Slocum leaned against the horse and got the leg raised. His eyebrows rose. "You've got sharp eyes. The shoe's coming loose."

"Looks as if you'da lost that there shoe in a day or two out in the hills. Real rocky travelin' from this point on, no matter what direction you head."

"Is there a farrier who can tend to it?"

"That'd be my brother," the stable man said. "He'll be back in an hour or so. He kin git right to it. Fer another five."

Slocum dickered some more and paid three dollars to have his mare reshod. With so much money riding high in his shirt pocket, he fought over the price as if it mattered out of pure habit. Most times, five dollars would be a week's pay.

"There a restaurant in town worth the name?"

"Cain't say there is. You might git some victuals down at the Lone Star Emporium. Ole Man Justin's kinda cheap when it comes to puttin' out food, but he don't poison nobody with it when he does. The Lone Star's the last decent saloon 'fore you git to Bitter Springs. From Bitter Springs you kin git north to New Mexico in a day or two, and we all know they don't have no good waterin' holes up there."

"Reckon not," Slocum said, not wanting to argue the point.

Slocum left his horse in the stable man's capable hands and sauntered down the street. When he spotted the stagecoach office, he veered across the dusty street and went inside. A bespectacled clerk slept, his head resting on his crossed arms as he sat behind a desk.

Slocum did not bother waking the man. Instead, he poked around, looking for wanted posters or some evidence a stage had been robbed. There was no reason a stagecoach had come from Sidewinder—or was coming here—when it lost its strongbox, but there was a chance that news of such a robbery would be posted all along the company's route.

A nail had been driven into a post and used to hold a dozen sheets of paper. Slocum slowly worked his way through them, hunting for any mention of a robbery or a reward for the return of the strongbox. All he found were scribbled notes he could not read and what appeared to be receipts for boarding the teams of horses used by the stage company. A smile came to his face when he saw that he had gotten a good rate over at the livery stables.

The clerk's snoring suddenly turned to a snort. The man stirred, pushed his glasses up his nose, and went back to sleep without ever seeing Slocum. Satisfied that he could find nothing about a robbery, and still wondering where the strongbox and all the money came from, Slocum left the office to go to the Lone Star Emporium. As he pushed through the saloon's doors, he felt the intense heat billowing outward. He had thought it was hot on the desert, and stifling as he rode between the towering canyon walls to reach Sidewinder, but this place was only an inch away from being on fire.

He went to the bar and leaned on it. It took a few seconds to get the barkeep's attention. The short, mousy man came over. Beady eyes fixed on Slocum.

"You got the look of a man wantin' a beer."

"It's too damn hot in here," Slocum said. "Why do you keep the stove all stoked up like that?"

"Good fer business. Warm beer's a nickel. Cold is a dime."

"You just sold me on a cold one then," Slocum said. "What'd it take for you to stop throwing wood on the stove?"

"More'n you got, mister."

Slocum took the mug and pressed his fingers against it, expecting it to be hot. To his surprise the beer was icy cold.

"Get ice from up north at Las Vegas," the barkeep said. "Pay through the nose for it, you gotta believe, but it's worth it."

"Adds a penny to the cost?" Slocum guessed. That gave the saloon an extra four cents profit for the same brew. He lifted the cold beer and drank it slowly, steadily, until only foam remained on the mug rim. He had another waiting for him before he put the glass down on the bar.

"You got a good head for business. Might be you'd like a job? Got another shift as barkeep to fill."

"Not bouncer?" Slocum sipped more slowly at the beer, wanting it to last. All the way down his gullet, it left a cold trail that spread throughout his body and made him feel more alive than he had since he'd ridden out into the hot West Texas desert days earlier.

"No call fer a bouncer." The barkeep jerked his thumb in the direction of four men coming into the saloon. Slocum looked and was sorry he did. All four sported badges. "Texas Rangers," the barkeep explained. "Got 'em comin' 'n goin' all the time. Nobody's gonna fool around them."

"A whole company? That's a powerful lot of law for a tiny town like Sidewinder."

"We don't mind. 'Bout the only business this town's got left, other than bein' on the sole route north through the Guadalupe Mountains. They spend their pay and keep things real quiet."

"Why so many?" Slocum asked again.

"Apaches," the barkeep said, looking sour. "Cain't git rid of them redskins no matter how we try. Put 'em on a reservation and they're off 'fore you can blink an eye. If it ain't Nana, it's Victorio and his witch sister Lozen. I hear tell she fights like a man and has the sight."

"The sight?"

"She kin tell where the enemy is. And Nana—he's older than dirt—he can find guns and ammo jist by holdin' up his hands. They get all red and hot when he's pointed in the right direction. Magical, they are. And too dangerous to ever tangle with."

"Unless you've got a company of Texas Rangers to back you up."

The barkeep laughed and said, "Nope. Better to *follow* 'em than lead 'em."

He scurried off like a rat to serve the four Rangers.

Slocum did not want to give the appearance of hurrying, but he was getting antsy having four Rangers in the same room with him. He wasn't the kind to sweat when he got into a tight spot, but he felt his shirt sticking to his whip-cord muscular torso because of the stove pouring out its heat. Finishing his beer, he started for the door, but a cold voice froze him in his tracks.

"Where you think you're goin', mister?"

Slocum turned slowly and faced the four Rangers seated at a table near the door.

"Got to check on my horse, if it's any business of yours, Ranger."

"Don't go lettin' Slim here get your goat, mister. Come on over. Pull up a chair." Another Ranger kicked out and sent a chair sliding in Slocum's direction. A dozen things raced through his mind and none of them ended well. The one with the least trouble attached to it convinced Slocum he ought to take the chair and bluff his way through.

"That's mighty neighborly of you," Slocum said, swinging the chair around and sitting on it, a little farther from the table than any of the Rangers.

"Justin, bring our friend another beer."

"A cold one," Slocum added. He waited to see the Rangers' reaction. He relaxed a little when they laughed.

"You ain't been in Sidewinder long but you figgered out Justin's game, eh? Good fer you." The Ranger named Slim laughed even more at this. "He's a wheeler-dealer, Justin is. We all reckon he keeps this place hot, not to sell more whiskey, but so his customers'll know what hell feels like."

"Then they'll feel right at home when Justin serves 'em there," finished another.

Slim looked hard at Slocum, who did not flinch.

"You got the look of a man I knew once. You ever been down in San Antone?"

"A time or two," Slocum said. "I just came from punching cattle for the Double Cross north of Fort Worth."

"How's Benton doing?"

Slocum shook his head sadly. "That's why I rode on. Fever killed a considerable number of his herd. Storms killed even more. Benton's balancing on the edge of losing everything."

"Pity," said Slim. "I was just over in that direction. Things are 'bout as grim as you make 'em out."

Slocum knew he had established his bona fides. Now he just wanted to finish his third beer and clear out.

"You come from the direction of the Pecos? Of course you did," Slim rambled on without waiting for Slocum's answer. "You see a gang of men anywhere along the road?"

"A gang? You looking for road agents?"

"The worst," said another of the Rangers. He leaned forward, forearms on the table, and leaned close as if he was sharing a secret. "You ever heard of the Rebel Jack Holtz Gang?"

Slocum had played enough poker to keep his face emotionless. Or at least he hoped so, since all four of the Rangers watched him like hawks. He took a sip of the cool beer, put it down on the table, then nodded slowly.

"Reckon I have. That's one mean hombre."

"Sooner kill you as talk to you," Slim said. "How'd you hear about Rebel Jack?"

Slocum shrugged. "Word gets around. It might have been something Mr. Benton said about rustlers."

"Rebel Jack's a rustler and a robber and a stone-cold killer. I'd as soon go up against an Apache war chief as him." Slim kept his eye on Slocum, waiting and watching for a mistake.

And Slocum knew why he was getting this treatment. Not only was he a stranger in Sidewinder, he had a well-worn six-shooter slung at his hip where he could get to it in a hurry. He looked like a gunfighter to these lawmen. And if he was a gunfighter, he might be one of Rebel Jack's men come to taunt the Rangers on their doorstep.

"No wonder you've got an entire company of Rangers here in Sidewinder," Slocum said. "Wish you luck catching him and his gang."

"You didn't see *any*thing out of the ordinary ridin' up?" The Ranger doing the questioning now sat across the table from Slocum and had both hands under the table. Slocum tried to remember how the lawman wore his six-shooter. If it was slung at his right hip, dragging it out in a hurry would be hard.

"Buzzards," Slocum said. "Spotted some circling my back trail. Nothing more than that." He finished his beer, then asked, "Has there been a stage robbery lately?"

"Why do you ask?"

"Saw what might have been a strongbox from a stage alongside the road. It had been rifled."

"You checked on it real careful, did you?"

"Didn't need to dismount to see that it was broken open and empty," Slocum said. "I poked around over at the stage office, but the clerk was asleep. Hated to wake a man in this heat."

Slim laughed and slapped Slocum on the shoulder. "You're all right, mister. What's your name?"

Slocum considered what to do. He had more than one wanted poster following him across the West. When he had returned to Slocum's Stand after the war, he had been shot up and badly needed time to recuperate. His parents had died and his brother Robert had been killed during Pickett's Charge. All Slocum had left in the world was one fine farm—until a carpetbagger judge had taken a fancy to it. No taxes had been paid, the judge lied. He and a hired gun had ridden out to seize the property.

They had gotten a patch of dirt, all right. Six feet deep each, down by the springhouse. Slocum had ridden away, never looking back. Killing a federal judge, even a no-account Reconstruction judge, was not a crime easily forgotten. Wanted posters for the killing had dogged his steps ever since. And truth to tell, he had added a few more for other crimes that he was not particularly proud of but that had kept him alive.

Had these Rangers seen one of those wanted posters? Slocum had rewards ranging from a few dollars up to a thousand on his head. From their reputation, Texas Rangers didn't care much about the money. They brought in their quarry for the sheer enjoyment of a job well done.

Before Slocum could respond to the question about his name, he looked up and saw trouble come through the saloon doors.

"I'll tell you what his name is," growled another Ranger. "It's dog meat!" The Ranger went for his pistol at the same instant Slocum kicked out and upset the table, sending beer flying through the air and momentarily taking out Slim and his three companions from the fracas.

Slocum drew with lightning speed and got off a shot that sent splinters from the table flying through the air. The

Ranger in the doorway never flinched. Slocum cursed himself for not checking closer to be sure the lawman had been dead back at the watering hole. The sight of a Ranger badge all buckled up and smeared with lead told the story.

Slocum had drilled the Ranger directly over the heart—but his badge had stopped the .36-caliber bullet from killing. Now Slocum was faced with a Ranger madder than a wet cat and willing to stand his ground and shoot it out.

Another shot finally forced the Ranger to give ground, but Slocum knew time was running out for him. The other four were getting their wits about them.

"What 'n hell's going on, Jeffers?" Slim pulled the table over and crouched behind it as he called to the Ranger in the doorway.

"That son of a bitch ambushed me. Shot me and left me for dead out at the watering hole," Jeffers said. "Nobody's gettin' away with that!"

The Ranger emptied his six-shooter at Slocum, firing with unwanted accuracy. Two of the bullets scored shallow grooves on Slocum's back and hip. Another missed his head by a hair and drilled a hole through both the brim and crown of his Stetson.

Slocum got off a couple more shots as he scuttled like a crab toward the rear of the saloon. Only when he reached the door to a storeroom did he stand, aim, and fire. Jeffers folded like a bad poker hand, clutching his belly. The other four turned their attention to the wounded Ranger, giving Slocum the time he needed to duck out of the barroom and into the storeroom.

He never slowed as he made a beeline for the barred rear door. He flung off the locking bar and burst out into the chilly evening. His clothing clung tenaciously to his body, glued to his skin by sweat from the incredible heat inside the saloon—or was it fear that made him sweat so much? Making enemies of Texas Rangers was never a good idea. One of them would track to the ends of the earth to make an arrest. Five of them—or possibly only four—would be a hundred times worse.

Slocum ran to the livery and looked around. The stable man was nowhere to be seen. Not even checking to see if the loose shoe had been renailed, Slocum saddled and mounted, getting the hell out of Sidewinder. There were only two ways he could go in the narrow canyon. Deeper into the Guadalupe Mountains, or back the way he had ridden earlier in the day. Knowing what lay out on the desert made the decision easy.

He galloped northwest, hoping he could find somewhere to hole up until the Rangers tired of hunting for him. Slocum worried that might be when hell froze over—or the Lone Star Emporium's stove was put out.

3

Slocum knew he could not ride the trail much longer and hope to evade the Rangers. He ran his horse until the mare began to tire, then slowed and led the horse off the trail into a rocky field. Circling, moving around to confuse the trail, Slocum made certain he left no trace behind by the time he tethered his horse in a stand of stunted oak trees on a rise and sat, rifle across his lap, to watch his back trail. He was more than fifty yards off the road and had done all he could to disappear. If the Texas Rangers found him, he would have no choice but to shoot it out with them.

Slocum wasn't too inclined to think the result would be to his benefit if it came to that.

He stood when he heard the steady clop-clop of hoofbeats on the road below him. He moved behind a tree trunk, balanced the rifle on a low limb, and waited. Sucking in his breath when the first Ranger appeared, he forced himself to be calm. If he shot too early, he could kill this Ranger, but how many rode with him?

Slocum blinked twice when he saw the second Ranger. It was Jeffers. The man rode bent over as if his belly hurt like hell—and it ought to. Slocum had shot him in the stomach. But then he had shot him in the heart before and the Ranger had lived.

"Son of a bitch," Slocum muttered under his breath. "That man's got more lives than a cat."

Two more Rangers trailed Jeffers. He would be up against four of them. Where the fifth one had gotten off to was something of a mystery. He didn't see the one named Slim anywhere. He might have remained in Sidewinder, or he might be riding parallel to the road hoping to flush Slocum.

Even if he had been inclined to shoot the other four in cold blood, Slocum knew better than to take them on without knowing where the fifth Ranger was. He hunkered down and waited for twilight to fade entirely and night to cloak him from sight. It got mighty cold mighty fast in the mountains, but Slocum could not build a fire without giving himself away.

He prowled about, hunting for a spot where he could see farther along the road. When he finally found such a spot atop a large boulder, he flopped down on his belly and saw the tiny orange dot of a campfire blazing in the distance. The Rangers had made camp. He knew they would be eating about now. His mouth watered at the thought of food— any kind of food.

Slipping back down the rock, he carefully retraced his way to where his horse cropped at tough grass growing around the base of the oak trees. He worked through the contents of his saddlebags until he found some jerky. That, along with water from his canteen, was all he dared eat. Taking his saddle blanket, he propped himself up against a rock and finally fell asleep some time later, only to come awake with a start.

It took him a few seconds to realize he had slept all night long, and the sun was poking up over a distant peak to shine in his face.

"What'll it be?" he asked his mare. "Stay here a spell longer or get back on the trail?" The horse looked at him with big brown eyes that told him nothing.

Slocum found one last hunk of jerky and ate it for breakfast, then set out to climb higher on the mountainside.

An hour of effort brought him to a point where he could see a goodly stretch of the trail winding around toward town. No trace of the Rangers in either direction made him uneasy.

"Where'd you get off to? Did you go back to Sidewinder? Or farther along the trail, wherever it leads?" Slocum got no answers to his questions. A mistake now would land him in the hoosegow—or worse. Ranger Jeffers might decide that being shot twice was enough for immediate execution.

Sitting in the fissure of a large rock protected him from sight and gave a limited view of the trail leading out of Sidewinder. Slocum sat most of the day, fuming at the lack of travel along the road. He might have missed the Rangers returning to their company headquarters. If he hadn't, he would ride into the four lawmen's arms—and guns—trying to escape. Only when the sun began dipping down low behind him did Slocum stir, stretch his aching limbs, and return to where his horse looked at him curiously. It had been a long time since there had not been a full day on the trail.

He saddled the horse and swung up, determined to get the hell out of here. Once more on the road, he glanced back in the direction of Sidewinder, then turned away and began the slow trek uphill into the heart of the Guadalupe Mountains. Every sense alert, Slocum passed the spot where the Rangers had camped the night before. He kept riding. Slocum tried not to jump at each small sound in the night, but he was keyed up. Only when he came to a fork in the trail did he relax. A signpost pointed to the west.

Slocum thought on the matter for a few minutes, then took the road leading west rather than the narrow rut going deeper into the mountains. The road here was wide and well traveled, telling him of considerable traffic occurring between Bitter Springs and Sidewinder. The Rangers would go to Bitter Springs because they'd think he would head for a town, but it also gave him a chance to get much-needed supplies. His belly grumbled, and a taste of whiskey would set good at the moment. As much as Slocum valued his scalp more than he did his belly, he would die if he did not get supplies before setting out across the desert he knew lay on the far side of the valley stretching all the way to El Paso.

Getting out of the maze of mountain canyons would go a long way toward giving him more freedom of travel. If the Rangers found a canyon mouth and simply put a sentry out, they could bottle him up for easy capture. At least out on the desert to the south, he had more choices about which direction to run, even if it was hotter than hell and twice as dry.

The road straightened out, and the mountains seemed to melt away as he entered a broad, grassy valley. He still had no idea where he was headed, but the road here was even better traveled than up around the signpost pointing to Bitter Springs. A large town would let him get the supplies he needed without the risk of being noticed.

The sun poked up over the hills about the time he realized his horse was starting to hobble along.

He jumped down and examined the loose shoe. Only two nails held it on.

"Looks like we'll both we walking for a while," Slocum said. "At least there's got to be a farrier where we're going, wherever that is."

He led the horse off the road to a thick stand of trees. Nestled in the center was a small pool of muddy water.

"Better than nothing," he told the horse, letting the mare drink her fill. Slocum used his bandanna to filter most of the dirt out as he drank. Then he went hunting, bagged a rabbit, and skinned and gutted it. His fire had finally settled down to decent cooking coals when he heard the pounding of hooves out on the road.

Slocum reached for his six-shooter, then relaxed. The sound was too loud for only four riders. This sounded like a dozen or more riders. If the Rangers had brought in the rest of their company to hunt for him, Slocum would have to do some fancy escaping. He balanced the stick holding the rabbit over the coals, then went to investigate.

Staying behind a tree, he peered out at the road. He had been right about the number of riders. A squad of cavalry troopers raced past, their banner fluttering. So many soldiers looking this fresh meant that Slocum was heading toward an army post. He slipped back to his breakfast, eating the half-cooked rabbit slowly. No matter what he did, he worked his way into troubles worse than those he fled.

He touched the wad of greenbacks in his shirt pocket. His trouble had begun when he took the money from the strongbox. Two soldiers and a Texas Ranger had ignited a prairie fire around him. Slocum finished the rabbit, then kicked dirt over the coals. If he rode into the fort, he might not be in any trouble. Two dead soldiers told no tales. It was quite likely the officers did not even know their men were dead, and if they did, nothing linked Slocum to their killing.

"Rebel Jack Holtz is prowling around," Slocum said aloud. "Might be he and his gang killed a pair of soldiers. Yeah." Slocum washed his hands off in the muddy pond, spent a few more minutes straining dirt from the water and filling his canteen, then mounted and rode in the direction of the fort.

Less than twenty minutes' ride took him to a rise looking down into the valley where the fort stretched out like a crazy quilt. A farm to one side grew corn, irrigated by an acequia coming down from the higher elevations. Like most forts in the region, the wall around the fort was hardly knee-high. Slocum guessed it was designed to keep in poultry rather than protect against Indians. A small cluster of buildings outside the low wall housed the fort's officers and their families. Slocum knew there would be a whorehouse there, too, but he was less interested in feminine companionship than he was in getting back on the road leading into the West Texas desert.

As pleasant as this place looked, he felt the hot breath of Texas Rangers on his neck.

Starting down the slope for the fort, he was startled by the shouted command for him to throw up his hands.

He glanced to the left side of the road and saw a soldier lying prone and peering down the long barrel of his rifle.

To the right stood a pair of soldiers. Both of them had their rifles trained on him, too. Caught in a cross fire, he could never escape.

"What's the problem?" Slocum called, doing as he was ordered.

"You got the look of an outlaw about you," claimed one soldier. "We're takin' you in to the fort."

Slocum's jaw tensed when he remembered the greenbacks in his pocket. What cowboy rode with that kind of money? He would have to make them believe he won it in a card game. But then he would have to explain why the men in the poker game had so much money. If he lied about where he had won the money, they would know. Never having been to Bitter Springs, he would have to claim Sidewinder—or somewhere else. Fort Worth? All this flashed through his head in a second. It wasn't a good lie, but it would have to do.

"Was heading that way," Slocum said, starting to lower his hands.

"Git 'em up. You're under arrest."

"For what? Riding along a road and—"

"Shut up. Two soldiers out of Fort Suddereth have gone missin'. We think they was shot down by outlaws."

"Do you stop every rider and accuse him of killing your men?" Slocum snorted in disgust.

"Ain't many travelers who aren't outlaws," said another soldier.

"Toss over your hogleg," ordered another.

"How do I do that if I've got my hands in the air?" Slocum looked around as an idea formed. If they took him to the cavalry post, they would likely decide he was responsible for killing the two troopers. There wouldn't be any evidence, but Slocum saw how touchy the men were. Evidence meant little when they were out for revenge. That he had actually shot and killed the two soldiers was purely incidental.

"Don't go mouthin' off," shouted the one who had been flat on the ground. He got up. The instant his rifle lowered,

Slocum used his knees to turn his horse. He applied his spurs and the mare bolted, jumping over the soldier's head and hitting the ground at a dead gallop directly behind him.

Keeping low, Slocum gave them no target. That did not stop the soldiers from firing at him. From his quick look around before lighting out, he had not seen where the soldiers had tethered their horses. This close to the fort, they might have been dropped from a wagon to stand guard. If so, Slocum was in luck. Finally. They could never follow him on foot.

Rather than swing around and head for the fort, he turned north toward Bitter Springs. He might be riding into the guns of the Texas Rangers, but he had no other choice. Off the road and riding into the countryside, he quickly found that his mare was not able to keep up the pace he wanted. Slowing, then stopping, he dismounted and saw the worst had happened. The horse had finally thrown the loose shoe. If he tried riding now, the horse would pull up lame and strand him for the soldiers—or the Rangers.

He looked around and cursed. The mountains to his east promised some sanctuary. Not much maybe, but more than he had out in the broad valley holding the fort. To the north lay Bitter Springs deeper in the Guadalupe Mountains, but he had no idea how many miles that was. If he returned to the road, he could make better time on foot, but he also ran the risk of being caught by the cavalry troopers galloping up and down the road.

Patting the mare, he saw no way out but to abandon the horse and set out on foot. But he could not do it. The horse would find enough to graze on in this valley and if he kept the horse with him, he was a sitting duck. It would be harder to cover his tracks. Any cavalry post out in Indian country had to have expert trackers. If the sentries along the road reported and the officer in charge decided, Slocum might find a half-dozen Apache scouts sniffing out his trail. A horse that had lost a shoe would leave a distinctive track.

"Come on," Slocum said, tugging on the reins. Something

would occur to him. Until it did, he was not setting his horse free.

He did the best he could to walk over rocky patches and find terrain where his tracks would be quickly erased by the feeble hot wind blowing through the valley. Dragging a clump of greasewood added an extra measure of protection from his tracks being found. But Slocum knew it wouldn't matter if a patrol spotted him.

By sundown, he had not seen any soldiers on his trail and angled toward the road. Dangerous though it might be, Slocum had no other choice if he wanted to get north to Bitter Springs. He and his horse walked along slowly until he heard the sound of horses coming from the direction of the fort. Quickly leaving the road, he went down in a draw out of sight. The horses slowed and then halted.

Slocum left his horse and ran down the draw, coming back around to a spot where he could see the road.

It looked mighty bleak to him. A squad had halted and the sergeant leading the soldiers pointed in the direction Slocum had taken. They had spotted his tracks. He reached for his six-shooter, but halted when he heard someone coming up behind him.

"They got you—unless you want to go along with me," a deeply resonant voice boomed out.

Slocum rolled over and saw a man dressed in a black cutaway coat and a threadbare vest staring at him. A tall silk stovepipe hat made him look ten feet tall, but Slocum guessed he was hardly six feet, and probably several inches less.

"Who might you be?" Slocum asked.

"No time for that. Do they know you by sight?"

"Ran into three sentries along the road earlier today. They got a good look at me."

The man nodded, chewed his thumb for a moment, then brightened.

"It's going to be hard for them to identify you in the dark, even if they saw you earlier. Give me your gun belt and hat. And strip off your coat and shirt. It's easier to remember a shirt than a face."

Slocum considered his plight. The man, if he had been armed, could have back-shot him and never bothered with any charade. A quick move got his gun and holster off. He sailed his bullet-holed hat to the man, and then quickly added both his coat and bloodstained shirt. When the cold night air hit his bare skin, his shallow wounds ached and made movement difficult.

"Come along, uh, come along, Jethro."

"Jethro?" Slocum laughed.

"It's as good a name as any. It's not your real name, is it? Good. No point letting them have too many clues." The man headed toward the draw and kept moving along it. The draw widened onto a dry flood plain. Slocum saw a large peddler's wagon parked ahead. The man in the stovepipe hat hurried to the rear of the wagon and tossed Slocum's gear inside. He pointed to a wheel, then put his finger to his lips cautioning Slocum to silence.

Slocum knelt by the wheel and examined it. Two spokes were coming loose. He began working on them with tools already laid out on the ground as the squad of soldiers rode up.

"Who're you?" demanded the sergeant at the head of the column.

"Why, sir, I am a man of the cloth, a man of God. I bring my ministry to those who cannot find the Gospel in remote towns. I am Daniel Whitmore, known far and wide as Preacher Dan."

With a flourish, Whitmore doffed his hat and bowed deeply.

"What's your business?"

"Why, Sergeant, I am bringing the word of the Lord to the people."

"What are you doing out on the road right now?" the soldier asked angrily.

"My handyman, Jethro, is struggling to maintain the integrity of my vehicle."

"What?"

"The wheel's coming off," Preacher Dan said tiredly. "It is a godsend that your men have come by so they can lend a hand."

"We're huntin' for a man responsible for killin' two soldiers."

"Your hunt can continue after you lend a hand. Remember the parable of the Good Samaritan."

"Where are you heading?"

"Why, we are going toward Bitter Springs. We have just visited Fort Suddereth."

"I seen 'im, Sarge," said a private. "He was run out of the fort by Captain Gunnison while you was out on patrol down south."

Slocum tensed. It was possible the sergeant had discovered the two dead soldiers rather than assuming they were dead because they had not returned. The commander at the fort seemed to prefer dropping off guards along the road rather than having them patrol on horseback.

"How many was with the preacher man?"

"Him an' another. I only heard of 'em. I was in the stockade fer—"

"Never mind," the sergeant said. "Patrol, ride!"

Slocum remained bent over the wheel until the soldiers had trotted off into the dark. Only when the dust had settled did he stand and wipe off his hands.

"Your wheel's fixed," he told Preacher Dan.

"Do tell. You are quite handy—as well as a murderer." The preacher did not sound as if he was frightened at the prospect.

"It was self-defense, and I'm not sure they were soldiers," Slocum said. "They wore uniform jackets, but nothing else about them spoke of the cavalry. Might be they killed the soldiers and took their uniforms." Slocum started to add "and looked for the loot from the stagecoach," but he held his tongue.

"That is between you and your conscience," Preacher Dan said. "I'm only pleased that you can fix things."

"I'm obliged you gave me the chance," Slocum said.

"And I'm glad he gave you the chance to take off your shirt," came a voice as soft and smooth as silk. "I certainly enjoyed the chance to see you half-naked."

Slocum turned and faced a dark-haired woman about as pretty as he had ever seen.

"Jethro, meet my daughter Tessa," said Preacher Dan Whitmore.

4

Slocum looked straight into the woman's bright blue eyes and saw the humor dancing there.

"You've got my horse," he said. Tessa led the mare, allowing it to hobble along at its own pace.

"And you've got . . ." Tessa's eyes dipped to Slocum's crotch.

"What?" Slocum asked.

"Dirty. Did you fix the wheel for Papa?"

"He did a right smart job of it, daughter," Preacher Dan said. "I knew the Lord would provide."

Slocum did not hear all of what Tessa replied but caught ". . . helps herself."

She handed the reins to Slocum. Their hands touched for a moment longer than necessary. Tessa was in no hurry to pull back, and neither was Slocum. She went around the wagon and opened the rear door, grabbed his shirt, and tossed it to him.

"It gets cold out in the desert. You'll need this to keep you warm—if you don't have other ways of doing so." Her bold stare challenged Slocum. He looked from her to Preacher Dan, who seemed oblivious to the byplay. Slocum doubted he was the first man Tessa had been so open with. He wondered if anything bothered the preacher. He had not blinked when Slocum confessed to killing two soldiers, and now he pointedly looked the other way as his daughter propositioned a man she had only met a few minutes earlier.

"I'm obliged, but I had better clear out. I don't want you good folks to get into trouble."

"The cavalry is no problem," Preacher Dan said. "Their commander chased us off the post, so we are a known quantity to them. We are beneath their notice."

"Beneath their contempt, you mean, Papa," Tessa said. "They were *so* rude. The things they said about us were criminal."

"Turn the other cheek, dear," the preacher said. "We must travel on now that we have done all we could at Fort Suddereth."

Tessa laughed and caused Slocum to look around sharply. Something in their tone suggested their mission at the cavalry post had been something other than saving souls. What it might have been, he could not say. The interior of the wagon was almost bare, with only a few boxes carefully covered with tarps against the front wall.

She tossed Slocum his gun belt and pistol. He saw how her fingers lingered on the ebony handle. He settled the belt about his waist and went to see how his mare was faring.

"You won't get a mile before they find you," the preacher said. "Ride with us. We're heading to Bitter Springs."

"I heard," Slocum said. He dropped the mare's hoof. The horse could walk, but not carry his weight. Escaping this part of the country looked increasingly as bleak as the desert itself.

"We can let your horse walk alongside. You can ride inside the wagon out of sight. Nobody's going to poke around a preacher's wagon," Preacher Dan said.

"They get mighty forgetful about what they're doing if I talk to them. I just don't know why." Tessa struck a pose that took Slocum's mind off his predicament. He suspected she used her wiles on any man who rode by, not just on him.

"I should tell you it's not only the cavalry that's looking for me. There was a problem with a Ranger named Jeffers," Slocum said. "There's no easy way of clearing that matter up with half the Rangers from Sidewinder hunting for me, too."

"You killed a Ranger?" This caused both father and daughter to look a mite more concerned.

"Can't say it wasn't for lack of trying," Slocum said, gauging their expressions, "but he walked away from the shoot-out." He did not add that Jeffers had escaped getting one of Slocum's bullets poked through him not once but twice.

"You have been a busy boy," Tessa said. "If you didn't actually kill a Ranger, they won't hunt for long. They have other pressing matters to occupy them."

"The Warm Springs Apaches are free from their reservation over in Arizona," Preacher Dan said.

"Heard tell of an outlaw gang that interested the Rangers, too," Slocum said. "And no," he hurried on, "I'm not part of any gang."

"I think our friend Jethro might prove an asset to our travels, daughter. What do you think?"

"Oh, yes, Papa, a real asset."

Slocum jerked when he felt her hand on his ass. She was a forward woman, bolder than many Cyprians he had encountered in saloons. But Tessa always leavened her lewd winks or outright leering with a small, almost shy look. It was as if she practiced on being bold as brass and was not quite sure of herself.

Slocum was sure of one thing. She was about the prettiest woman he had laid eyes on in a month of Sundays. Tessa stood about five feet five, with everything in perfect proportion. While the gingham dress she wore was chaste enough, the way she wore it was not. Her breasts thrust out impudently against the fabric, and bounced delightfully as she turned this way and that. As she moved, she made sure her skirt swirled around her ankles, giving Slocum a hint of what lay beneath. It was enough to get his heart hammering faster. Most of all, it was the way she looked at him that made him respond so.

When she eyed him, he thought there was nothing else in the entire world but the two of them.

"Get on in the rear, Jethro," said the preacher. "It's time we rolled on to Bitter Springs."

"Go on, spread out a blanket, and get some sleep," Tessa said. "You're going to need all the rest you can get."

There wasn't much left to the imagination in the way she spoke or the look on her face. Slocum climbed into the rear of the wagon, and experienced a moment's pang when the door was shut and latched behind him. It was almost completely dark, and he fumbled about until he found his bedroll and spread it out in the small space left. He curled up and closed his eyes. He drifted off thinking of Tessa, and awoke with her face only inches from his.

"We're there," she said softly. "You keep inside the wagon for a spell. And leave that shooting iron of yours behind when you go out. You're a handyman, not a gunslinger."

She bent and gave him a quick peck on the cheek and then was gone. He sat up and fumbled around before making sure his Colt Navy and holster were hidden under his blanket. Only then did he push open the rear door and step out into the bright sun of day. Squinting, he estimated the height of the sun, and knew it must be close to ten in the morning. He had slept like a dead man all the way along a rocky road.

He dropped to the ground, scratched himself, and then walked around the wagon. For the first time, he read the sign painted on the side in large gold letters: PREACHER DAN'S ROLLING MINISTRY.

Slocum wondered if he could scrape off the paint and find evidence that Daniel Whitmore had been a dentist before or maybe a peddler of snake oil. Neither would have been too outrageous for Preacher Dan.

He looked around the town as he circled the wagon, checking to be sure the wheel was still intact. He shook it, and decided the wheel had to be taken off and fixed better

than he could do with it still on the axle. A wheelwright
would be best, though Slocum could do the repair work if
necessary. One thing he could not do without tools was
shoe the mare. He unfastened the reins where the horse had
been secured on their trip up from Fort Suddereth, and
tugged gently.

"Time to get you looked after all properlike," Slocum
said. The mare understood, and hardly hobbled as he led
her to the town stables. After a protracted amount of dick-
ering, Slocum arranged for both care and shoeing without
spending a fortune. Small-town businesses sometimes took
it into their heads to overcharge travelers.

"What about the other horse?" asked the liveryman.

"Other?" Then Slocum remembered he worked for
Preacher Dan as a handyman. "Oh, the one still at the
wagon," he said, covering his gaffe. "I'll bring her over in
a while. The preacher wanted to keep the rig ready to roll
so he could set up once and not have to move later."

"Makes sense," the man said. "Same price fer the second horse, 'cept it don't have to be shoed, does it?"

Slocum knew it did not. He almost asked about the
saloons in town—he had seen three on his way to the livery
stables—but caught himself in time. He had no idea what
kind of spiel the preacher gave. If it was about the evils of
Demon Rum, Slocum didn't want to ruin things by being
seen knocking back a few shots of whiskey.

"There you are, Jethro," Tessa called. "Papa wants the
wagon taken to the edge of town, out by the bank. You
know how to set it up." She looked around and smiled at
two women eavesdropping from the nearby boardwalk.
The women nodded brusquely and hurried away, whispering between themselves.

"Don't reckon you're always welcome in these towns. Is
there already a minister in Bitter Springs?"

"I couldn't say," Tessa admitted. "Papa usually comes to
an arrangement with any competition."

"Competition for souls or money?"

"What's the difference? As the Bible says, it's easier to

get a camel through the eye of a needle than it is for a rich man to enter the Kingdom of God."

"Matthew 19:24," Slocum said automatically.

"What?" Tessa looked at him suspiciously.

"The Bible quotation."

"Oh, yes, of course. You are a surprising man . . . Jethro."

"John," he said. "John Slocum."

"I like that better," Tessa said. She reached out and lightly brushed her fingertips across his stubbled cheek. "Get the wagon down to that empty lot across from the bank. I'll be down soon."

Slocum looked over the woman's shoulder, and saw two men come out of a saloon. The sunlight glinted brightly off their badges. Texas Rangers.

He turned suddenly and said over his shoulder, "I'll only get you in trouble if you're seen with me."

"Oh," Tessa said. "I thought they'd be inside for a while yet. They had half a bottle of whiskey on the table in front of them."

"You knew they were in town and didn't tell me?"

"Why bother you with something like that? Get into the back of the wagon, John. I'll drive down where Papa wants you to set up."

Slocum ducked into the back of the wagon and closed the door. The last look he got outside was of the pair of Rangers walking purposefully toward him. There wasn't any way of securing the door on the inside, and Slocum could not risk letting go of his grip on the handle to reach for his six-shooter. His muscles knotted with strain as he heard one Ranger call out, "Wait up. We want a word with you, ma'am."

Slocum almost let the door flop open so he could get his six-gun and shoot his way out of town. Tessa might tip off the lawmen that a desperado was lurking in the rear of her wagon, or she might inadvertently give him away.

"Why, if it isn't two big, strong Rangers. What can I do for such fine, upstanding God-fearing men?"

Slocum thought she laid it on too thick, but neither Ranger sounded put out.

"Ma'am, we seen you just pulled into town."

"That is true. Please, take this broadside. It explains everything. Preacher Dan will hold a tent meeting this afternoon."

"We're not interested in that," said the other Ranger. "Did you come across an hombre out on the trail?"

"Why, yes," Tessa said. Slocum strained to wrap a corner of his bedroll in his fingers. He tugged hard and brought it closer. His Colt slid with it.

"What's that noise?"

Slocum fumbled to wrap his hand around the ebony butt of his six-shooter before the Rangers poked their heads into the rear of the wagon.

"Why, nothing. We've had problems with a wheel rattling and wobbling on us."

"The man you spotted outside town? What about him?"

"There were four of them, Ranger," she said. "They said they were from Fort Suddereth. They wore uniforms and all, so we just assumed they were telling the truth. That's always the best policy, don't you think? Believing people until you learn different?"

"Soldiers?" The Ranger sounded disgusted.

"One wore stripes. The others called him Sergeant, so we thought he was."

"Nobody else? A solitary rider?"

"It's mighty lonely out on the road to Bitter Springs," she said wistfully. "I wish there had been someone else. Papa would have preached some Gospel to him." She chuckled. "I do declare, it gets mighty boring out there when I'm the only one he has to practice his sermons on."

That was the right thing to say. The Rangers promised they would look in on the revival meeting, but Slocum doubted they would unless they came solely to gawk at Tessa. He relaxed and placed his six-gun back on the floor just as the wagon lurched and sent him sprawling. The door swung open and then closed. He doubted the Rangers got a good enough look into the wagon to see him, but he got back to his feet and grabbed the handle to hold the door shut as they bounced along the rocky street.

Tessa finally pulled back on the reins and stopped the horse. She went around the wagon, rapped twice on the door, and said, "I forgot the password, John. Let me in."

Slocum relaxed his grip and the woman flowed into the back of the wagon like water over rock. She turned and dropped onto his bedroll, then yelped. She lifted herself off the blanket, reached under her, and came up with his six-shooter.

"You have strange bed companions, John."

He took it from her and put it aside.

"How strange are *you*?" he asked.

"As strange as you want," Tessa said, lying back. She reached up and began unbuttoning her dress until she could shrug her shoulders and get out of it. In the dim light filtering through cracks in the wagon, Slocum saw she was stripped to the waist. Her breasts seemed to glow with an inner light that drew him powerfully.

Reaching out, he took each soft mound in a hand and squeezed down. He was rewarded with a soft moan of pleasure.

"You know what I want, John. I didn't think you had gone around the bend."

He leaned over and lightly kissed one nipple. She arched her back and thrust her breast up into his face. He opened his lips enough to take more of the succulent mound of tit flesh into his mouth. His tongue worked fiercely on her nipple until it was rock hard and pulsing with need.

"That makes me so excited," she moaned out. Her fingers ran through his hair, holding his head down to her bosom. He lightly nipped at the rubbery tip and brought a cry of delight to her lips. She relaxed her hold on his head for a moment, allowing him to move quickly to her other quivering mound. He engulfed it with his mouth and sampled the taste before moving lower.

"Oh, oh!" Tessa squirmed as he licked down the deep

valley between her breasts to her heaving belly. As he kissed and tongued, he ran his hands down low to her legs and then up under her skirt to get it out of the way. His hands met only sleek, warm flesh—no undergarments.

This made Slocum harder by the second as he worked around to the inside of her thighs and then parted them. Rocking up and moving on his knees, he knelt between her wide-spread legs. He looked down into her eyes. Her eyelids had half-closed and the expression on her face was one of sheer raw desire.

"Let me," she said. Tessa struggled up and got her hands onto his waist. It took her a while to unbutton his fly and let his erection come sailing free, but it was worth the wait. Her fingers closed around his hardness and drew him forward and down.

"There," she said, holding the purpled knob of his cock against her nether lips. "I want it there." Her voice had turned husky.

The feel of her fingers on him and the nearness of her heated core drove Slocum onward. He caught himself on his hands on either side of her body as he stroked forward. For a moment, he thought he was going to have to work harder. Then she shifted her hips and he sank balls-deep into her tightness.

They both gasped then. For a moment, Slocum hung suspended, then recovered his senses enough to draw back gradually. The wetness and heat surrounding him almost robbed him of his control. He entered her again, this time more slowly, relishing the feel of her most intimate flesh against his length. When he was again fully within her, she squeezed down with her strong inner muscles.

"You're so big," she sobbed out. She clung to his arms and began thrashing about under him. The movement, the tightness, the heat all lit the fuse within Slocum. He began moving with more power and speed until friction threatened to burn him to a nubbin.

She cried and moaned as he moved still faster until

there was no turning back for him. The fire within his loins erupted. He arched his back and tried to split her in half, only to find she was writhing about beneath him, lost in her own wonderland of ecstasy.

Spent, Slocum sank forward until his weight pressed Tessa down to the wagon floor. She did not object. She began kissing his ear and stroking over his back.

Finally, he raised up and said, "People will wonder what we're doing in the wagon. We should go outside. Or you should. It'd be best for me to stay inside."

"Who cares what the people think? I've—" Tessa bit off her words and focused on him. "You're right, John. You'd better stay out of sight until we're sure the Texas Rangers have left town."

"The way you invited them to the revival means every last one of them will be here."

"What are you saying? That I might have flirted a little too much with them?"

"Something like that. It's one way to get a crowd, but I don't want them around."

"Really?" She grinned wickedly. "Afraid of a little competition?" She reached down between them and took his limp organ in her hand and began massaging it. Only a twitch or two rewarded her effort. "You don't have to worry about them. You did just fine."

Tessa scooted about and began getting back into her dress. Slocum sat on a box and buttoned himself up, then hefted his six-shooter.

"You don't have to use that on me," she said, her eyes sparkling.

"Let me know if the Rangers are outside. I hear a crowd already starting to gather."

"Oh, no, it's late!" she cried. "Papa will kill me if I don't get to work!"

With that, Tessa Whitmore slid past Slocum, gave him a quick kiss, then popped out of the wagon and went to work calling to those who were beginning to assemble. Slocum wondered what she considered her work to be, then settled down, six-gun in his hand, to listen to Preacher Dan's impassioned sermon that began fifteen minutes later.

All Slocum prayed for was the departure of the Texas Rangers from Bitter Springs.

5

The crowd dispersed after sundown. Slocum poked his head out to be sure the coast was clear, then dropped to the ground and walked around the wagon to where Preacher Dan and his daughter huddled together, splitting the take after passing the hat. Whitmore looked up and grinned from ear to ear.

"You bring us good luck, Jethro."

"John," Tessa said. "His name's John."

"That doesn't matter a whole lot," Preacher Dan said airily. "He's lucky, no matter what he calls himself."

"You see the Rangers anywhere in the crowd?" Slocum directed the question to Tessa, but Preacher Dan answered.

"Might have been one early on, but he drifted away before I got down to the serious preaching. From what I heard, the whole lot of them left for Sidewinder. There's been a sighting of Victorio, and the Rangers are trying to get the jump on the cavalry out of Fort Davis. Whoever captures that red devil will bask in the veritable light of public adoration for a whole long time."

"Bask in the light," muttered Slocum, shaking his head. "Highfalutin words that don't mean a thing if you get an Apache arrow in your back."

"Such is the sorry fate of too many defenders of the

public safety," Preacher Dan said pompously. He laughed and added, "It's more lucrative defending the public morals." A thick sheaf of greenbacks protruded from his coat pocket.

"Looks as if you've found your calling." Slocum turned to Tessa, who smiled angelically. He remembered the afternoon with her in the wagon when she was more than a tad devilish. That was the woman he preferred, though he wasn't going to tell her pa that.

"We're leaving the wagon parked here overnight. Tessa and I have rooms in the fine hotel. You're welcome to sleep inside the wagon."

"Don't mind if I do," Slocum said, knowing his usual place in the stables was likely to be a dangerous one if the Texas Rangers returned and stabled their horses. "I can watch over your belongings."

"Do that," Preacher Dan said a little uneasily. He extended his arm to his daughter and said, "Come along, Tessa. We must go preach some Gospel at the nearest place that serves a nice, big juicy steak."

"Papa, don't you think John could join us? We could pay."

Slocum saw the idea of him joining them for dinner was less worrisome to Preacher Dan than having to pay for it. He quickly assured her it would not be a good idea with the Rangers nosing around.

"This town supplies a considerable amount of goods for Fort Suddereth, too," Preacher Dan told Slocum. "Be careful if you explore. The sergeant you ran afoul of on the road might be here picking up this or that or ordering flour and the like."

Slocum nodded in agreement. The two walked off arm in arm. A momentary pang almost made Slocum call out and ask to join them. He had plenty of money, and it was burning a hole in his pocket. Touching the thick wad in his shirt pocket reassured him it was still waiting to be spent. Then he pushed aside any notion of doing that right now. Going to a saloon was foolhardy since that was the exact place a soldier or Ranger was most likely to be.

After making certain the wagon was secure, he walked to the edge of town and looked down the main street. Bitter Springs was much larger than Sidewinder, with a bank and three saloons and more businesses than he could shake a stick at. Sure that most of the town had either gone home or was gathered in the saloons, Slocum began a slow circuit to get the lay of the land. He felt immediately boxed in.

Sidewinder had been in the saddle between two mesas. Bitter Springs was similarly located, though there was only one mesa rising about a hundred feet above the rooftops of the tallest buildings. On the other side, a sheer cliff poked straight up and prevented Bitter Springs from expanding any way but along the rocky face. The tracks in the dirt told Slocum a considerable amount of freight came into the town every week. The ruts were deep, and the road well traveled.

He wandered about until he came to the hotel. Two windows were lit by lamps burning in the rooms. Slocum considered seeing if one of those might be Tessa's and if she'd waited up for him. As he watched, one light winked out. He stared at the other until it, too, was extinguished. Resigned to his lonely fate, Slocum turned back to the wagon and crawled inside, spread out his bedroll, and went to sleep thinking of Tessa.

His dreams eventually turned to less pleasant things. Texas Rangers shooting at him. Dead cavalry troopers. And a deadly, ghostly presence floating all around, always out of sight but nonetheless menacing. By the time he woke the next morning, he was already soaked in sweat. He was sitting cross-legged when Tessa opened the door and let in the heat from outside. Even in the middle of the mountains, summer in Texas was stifling.

"Come on, sleepyhead," she said brightly. "I need you to accompany me."

"Where?" Slocum reached for his six-shooter, but she shook her head.

"I need an escort to the bank. It's only across the street."

"If you've got the money from yesterday . . ." he began. His hand rested on his six-shooter. He felt vulnerable without it, and if Tessa wanted him to guard the money her pa had raised at yesterday's revival meeting, the gun would go further as a deterrence than his mere presence.

"It will be fine," Tessa finished for him. "Come along. The bank is just now opening its doors."

Slocum reluctantly left his gun belt behind in the wagon and hurried to catch up with Tessa. She was already halfway across the street and paying him little attention, as befitting a preacher's daughter with her pa's handyman. Slocum reached the bank in time to open the door for her.

"Should I wait outside, ma'am?" he asked.

Her eyebrows arched in surprise and she shook her head, then patted a stray lock of dark hair back into place as she brushed past him into the bank.

Slocum saw the tellers all look up when Tessa entered. A man behind a low railing hurried out to greet her.

"Good morning," Tessa said pleasantly. "Are you the banker I must see to open an account?"

Slocum stepped to the side and let the bank president make his introductions.

"I am so pleased you wish to do business with my bank. My name's Morton Thompson. Please, come this way and let's talk." Thompson ushered Tessa behind the railing to a chair in front of his large oak desk.

Slocum paid less attention to her and the bank president than he did to the safe behind them. It loomed large and black, made out of cast iron. The lock and handles were sturdy, but Slocum knew a few sticks of dynamite would blow off the door. Its weight prevented anyone from making away with it. Slocum bent over and tried to peer under the safe. It sat flat against what appeared to be a brick floor. If there had been legs, Slocum would have considered tipping the safe over and attacking it through the bottom. This made it impossible to do. For all he knew, there were bolts fastened to the safe and fixed into the floor.

Dynamite, he decided, was the best way to get into the safe if you were so inclined and did not have the combination.

He jerked his attention away from a robbery he would never commit to focus on what Tessa was saying.

"My father is so taken with this town, its people, its generosity, that he has decided to build a church here. A regular ministry would afford spiritual guidance for more than the few who could attend the services given by an itinerant preacher."

"A new church, eh? That will take a considerable amount of money. Bitter Springs is a boomtown and building materials are scarce. Scarcity means added expense."

"We know that, Mr. Thompson. We have a small deposit to start our church building fund. Can you accept such a small amount?" Tessa pulled out a thick wad of bills from her purse. Both Slocum and Thompson stared at the money. The bank president recovered quickly.

"I am sure we can deal with this sum, Miss Whitmore." Thompson took the money and counted it, then counted it once more before looking up with eyes wide. "This is a few dollars shy of a thousand."

"My father will want only the finest church for the people of Bitter Springs," she said sweetly. "If we deposit this, might we arrange for a building loan?"

"Of course," Thompson said without thinking. Then his banker's instincts came to the fore. "How much are we talking about?"

Slocum saw greed bring a slight flush to the banker's face when Tessa told him, "Five thousand more."

"The source of revenue will be from tithing?"

"Donations, tithing, services, although those will be smaller amounts."

"Services?"

"Weddings, funerals," Tessa said offhandedly. "We certainly hope there will be far more weddings—and baptisms—than funerals."

"Of course, that's what we all wish. Now, Miss Whitmore, let's fill out some paperwork and—"

Slocum ignored the rest of what Morton Thompson had to say. He was busy once more studying the building, how it was constructed, ways to rob the bank. If Thompson could promise so much money to a church building fund, he had to have a considerable amount more locked in his safe.

Slocum turned suddenly when the front door opened and three heavily armed men walked in. Slocum reached for his six-shooter and found only empty hip. Then he saw how the tellers greeted the trio. These were bank guards arriving late for work. He considered asking how often the guards were late. If he intended to rob the bank, it would have to be done prior to the guards' arrival in the morning.

He smiled just a little. He had no way of robbing the bank. The safe was secure, the guards were numerous, and he was all alone. Beyond this, he had plenty of money in his pocket. Still, it paid to keep his skills sharp and his mind active and on the lookout for opportunity.

Tessa rose, extended her hand, and presented it to Mort Thompson. For a moment, Slocum wondered if the man was going to shake her hand or kiss it. The bank president decided on shaking it, but he held on for a mite too long. Tessa did not seem to mind as she flirted outrageously with him. Then she pulled free. Slocum opened the gate in the railing for her, and followed her outside into the bright Texas sunlight.

He squinted as they crossed the street, then ducked behind the wagon as a squad of soldiers rode in from the north.

"There's no need to worry, John," she said. "The boys in blue aren't looking for you."

Slocum saw she was right, and she had not even given the soldiers a second glance. Somehow, she had taken it all in without breaking stride.

"They're depositing money in the bank to pay for Fort Suddereth's purchases. There will also be a considerable sum in gold to cover the fort's payroll."

He looked at her, wondering how she knew all this. She and her pa had just arrived in Bitter Springs. Rather than ask, he said nothing. He watched the soldiers intently as they dismounted and positioned themselves around the bank, two at each corner and three around back. In a few minutes, a heavily laden wagon arrived carrying four more alert soldiers. They drew up in front of the bank and hopped down. The driver and his assistant worked to unload heavy cases from the wagon while the others watched eagle-eyed as citizens passed by.

"Why do they use a bank in Bitter Springs rather than going on to the fort?" he asked.

"Politics. Mr. Thompson is a personal friend of the governor of this fine state. Keeping army payrolls, even for a short while, is a lucrative proposition for any bank." She laughed softly. "And for any banker. Our Mr. Thompson is quite the wheeler-dealer."

"You saying he uses the money for something other than paying army accounts?"

"Now, how could I possibly know such a thing, John?" She touched his cheek, then turned to leave. She stopped and did not look back at him as she said, "You would do well to find something to occupy your time. I do not recommend pursuing Demon Rum. It will be the death of you."

"You make it sound like I'm a drunkard," Slocum said.

"Gin mills can be dangerous places."

Slocum's rumbling belly told him he ought to get something to eat. Where better than the free lunch at a saloon? And where better than a saloon to overhear gossip? He felt currents flowing through Bitter Springs that he could not explain. His eyes going to the bank across the street ignited old hungers in him. In spite of the heavy safe and guards, the reward for breaking into that bank would be great. Moreover, he was already being chased by both the Texas Rangers and the cavalry. How many more lawmen could get on his trail? So many hunted him now, any more would bump into each other.

Tessa sashayed off, giving Slocum a good look at her hindquarters moving seductively. He wondered if the show was just for him or for any man who happened to notice. It hardly mattered. He appreciated the movement. When she vanished into the hotel, he got into the rear of the wagon and strapped on his six-shooter. Feeling dressed once more, he went to the nearest saloon.

He licked his lips, remembered what whiskey tasted like and how long it had been. The grumbles in his belly convinced him a beer or two along with some food would not pose much of a problem as long as he stayed in the background. At this time of day, there weren't likely to be many customers.

Slocum walked to the swinging doors, looked into the saloon, and then went inside. Two men played high-low at a table near the door. Neither bothered to even glance in his direction as he walked in.

He ordered a beer from the stocky man behind the bar. The barkeep looked to be fifty and moved with an arthritic shuffle. His one good eye was hardly in better condition than the milky, blind one.

Slocum helped himself to the fixings for a roast beef sandwich, slathered on a healthy dollop of mustard, and washed it down with the beer. He strained to eavesdrop on the two men playing cards, but they kept their voices low. He doubted they had much to say that he wanted to hear. The barkeep talked to himself all the time, and Slocum was certain he had no desire to hear more of the man's maundering.

After a second sandwich and beer, he'd started to leave when a man swung into the saloon as if he were king of all he surveyed. Slocum's eyes narrowed as he sucked in his breath and held it. The man wore his six-gun low on his left hip. He didn't have a right hand, and wore a battered CSA garrison cap pulled down on his scarred forehead.

Slocum's green eyes locked with the man's icy blue ones. The shock of recognition startled the one-handed man. Then he squared off and rested his hand on the side of his holster.

"Slocum," he snarled. "We got a score to settle."

6

"Been a long time, Toombs," Slocum said. "What was it? Just before the Lawrence raid?"

"Seems like yesterday to me, Slocum. You blowed my damn hand off. I missed all the fun Quantrill had fer us. And I never quit hatin' you!"

Slocum studied the man closely, looking for the slightest twitch that would signal that Toombs was going for the six-shooter at his hip. They had ridden together under William Quantrill, murdering and pillaging and trying to convince themselves this was the way war was fought. Leastways, Slocum had tried to convince himself until the lies and blood had piled up too much, even for a war-hardened captain like him. Killing Yankee soldiers was one thing, but he had become increasingly disaffected with wanton murder of civilians, and had drawn the line at massacring young boys in Lawrence, Kansas. Quantrill's brother had been killed, and he had exacted revenge by leaving more bodies to bury than there were people to bury them. Protesting the slaughter had gotten Slocum gut-shot by Quantrill's right-hand man, Bloody Bill Anderson.

But the uneasiness with them had started earlier, and Rufus Toombs had been a big part of that. He had pushed Slocum by calling him a gutless poltroon for his complaints.

51

No man got away with that. After a bare-knuckles fight had left Toombs bruised and bloody, he had slunk off. The kind of man Toombs was had come to the surface fast after the whupping. Slocum had blasted Toombs's gun hand off with a shotgun when the man tried to bushwhack him. After all these years, Toombs had not mellowed, and still groused about missing the chance to murder eight-year-olds who just happened to be in a Yankee-controlled town.

"You still the same back-shooting coward you always were, or have you grown a spine?" Slocum asked.

"I wasn't tryin' to shoot you in the back, damn you, Slocum. You snuck up on me with a shotgun. A *shotgun*! I never had a chance. You shoulda kilt me then and there 'cuz now I'm gonna kill you."

"Been practicing with your left hand, Toombs? If not, you'd better apologize. I hope you decide to go for your iron. You're right about one thing."

"What's that?" Toombs's hand began to twitch.

"I should have killed you on the spot back then. No tellin' how many lives you've taken since then. And you probably shot each and every one of them in the back."

Toombs went for his gun. Slocum was faster. And more accurate with his first shot. Toombs grunted as the slug ripped through his chest. He still managed to draw his gun, but it discharged into the floorboards, kicking up a pillar of dust and splinters. He dropped to his knees and fought to lift his six-shooter for another shot at Slocum.

"Die, damn you," Slocum said. This time he aimed for the man's head and did not miss. His bullet tore through Toombs's forehead. When the former Confederate soldier crashed to the floor, he was deader than a doornail.

The barkeep laid a pistol on the counter, stood on tiptoe, and looked at the body stretched out on his floor. "You two know each other?" he asked.

Slocum slid his Colt Navy back into his holster, glad he had taken the time to strap it on. Knowing Toombs the way he did, he knew he would have been dead if he had not been able to defend himself.

"Did once," Slocum said to the barkeep.

"I seen it all. He throwed down on you, mister. Another beer?"

Slocum saw that both cardplayers had disappeared. It would be only a matter of minutes before the town marshal showed up, waving his gun around and demanding to know what was going on. Slocum dared not be tossed in the town hoosegow for even a few hours. Any lawman worth his salt would ask around if his prisoner was wanted for anything else. Both the Texas Rangers and the army would end up fighting over Slocum, each wanting to stretch his neck.

"I'll take a rain check on that beer," Slocum told the barkeep.

At the doors leading out into the main street, he stopped and stared at the trio of men running toward him. The poker players must have alerted the three gunmen wearing Confederate caps similar to the one now drenched in Toombs's blood.

He backed away, then found the door at the rear of the saloon and left in a hurry. Slocum did not recognize the men coming to see what happened to their partner, but he knew their type. The hard expressions, the pistols slung at their hips, the Confederate regalia all told him they were likely riding on the wrong side of the law.

The hot sun burned at his face as he hurried to the stables. He saw half a dozen horses crowded into the stalls. Toombs and his partners had just come to town since these animals had not been here the day before.

"You come to check on yer horse?" The stable owner moseyed out of the tack room.

"Is the shoe nailed down again?"

"Surely is." The man looked at Slocum curiously. "That there's a saddle horse, not a draft animal."

"So?"

"I thought you used it to pull the preacher man's wagon. No way could that horse do a chore like that. Too high-spirited."

"I ride alongside most of the time. The other horse does the pulling. Is the mare fed and watered?"

"Groomed, too. You lookin' to doin' some explorin' around Bitter Springs?"

"Where's the road to the north go?" Slocum's mind raced as he considered what to do. He wished he had time to pay his respects to Preacher Dan and his lovely daughter—especially Tessa!—but he felt the jaws of a vise closing around him. As if the Rangers and the cavalry hunting for him weren't enough, he had killed an old enemy and had at least three killers on the other side of the law on his trail, too.

"Well," said the liveryman, scratching his chin thoughtfully, "if you veer on to the northeast, you can go to Frijole. Take the western branch, and you end up out on a dry salt lake. That way leads to Cornuda and on over to El Paso. Bad desert there, but that's the way most of the army shipments come, the ones not from Fort Union, that is."

"Thanks," Slocum said. He grabbed his saddle and threw it over the mare's back. The horse whinnied in complaint. It didn't take long to get used to standing around in the shade with all the food and water you could want. He rattled his canteen and held it up. "You fill this up for me?"

The stable owner looked at him curiously, then took it silently and went to fill it for Slocum. This gave Slocum the chance to whip out his knife and cut the cinch straps almost all the way through on the saddles of the four new horses. He tucked the blade back into the top of his boot when the man returned with the canteen.

"All full. You might want to take a canvas desert bag, too. Gives a taste of cooler water."

Slocum began to get antsy about leaving. The man seemed intent on jawing.

"If you've got one handy, I'll buy it," Slocum said.

"Over at the general store, they got a couple. My brother owns the store," he said, as if this made the suggestion on the level.

"Won't be gone that long," Slocum lied. It would take an hour for the Rebs to repair their saddle cinches. That would give Slocum a little head start. Casting doubt about where he headed might give him a few more minutes if they waited for him to return.

"I can surely understand that," the man said. He grinned almost shyly. "That daughter of the preacher man, she's a real peach."

"That she is," Slocum said. He swung into the saddle and rode around the back way to Preacher Dan's wagon. It took Slocum only a few seconds to grab his bedroll and other items he had stashed there. Pausing a moment, he stared over at the hotel, not sure if he ought to risk going to say good-bye to Tessa. From the ruckus being kicked up at the saloon, he decided he had better get on the trail or he would be in the middle of a new war.

Regretting it, he turned his back on Tessa Whitmore and trotted out of town, heading north. He remembered what the stable owner had said when he reached a fork in the road after riding a half hour. Due west stretched a dry lake bed, and to the northeast was another town called Frijole. Having had his fill of beans, Slocum went westward and immediately regretted it.

The hills began to flatten out fast. From his position along a higher elevation in the road, he spotted a dust cloud being kicked up out on the flats.

"Damn," he muttered. Reaching back into his saddle-bags, he pulled out a pair of field glasses and put them to his eyes. His fear was realized. Through the dust and heat shimmer rising from the arid land, he made out a column of cavalry troopers. He put the field glasses back into his saddlebags and wheeled about. Frijole didn't seem like such a bad spot after all.

Nowhere along the road from the fork afforded any real cover. He considered finding an arroyo, getting down into it, and hoping the soldiers rode on past him. Taking such a risk, though, was not something he wanted to do unless absolutely necessary. He galloped back into rockier country, the mountains rising all around by the time he reached the road to Frijole.

He turned northward, and had ridden hardly a mile when he began to get an itchy feeling at the back of his neck. This section of the road ran through rocky terrain that could provide a fair amount of cover. Slocum decided it was time to rest his horse and get rid of the uneasy feeling that grew with every step he took toward Frijole.

Dismounting, he led the mare through a maze of rocks, and finally found a sandy spit behind some boulders. It was hotter than hell here, the rocks trapping the burning summer heat, but Slocum was in no mood to hunt for a better rest area. He lashed the horse's reins to a mesquite bush where the mare could graze on some beans. His mouth like cotton, he sampled some of the water in his canteen and almost spat it out.

Wherever the stable man had filled it had been polluted. Slocum reckoned that was the man's way of getting him over to the general store to buy a desert bag. Wiping the water all over his face relieved some of the heat and got rid of trail dust. As Slocum hung the canteen back on his saddle, he heard the steady thunder of approaching horsemen.

Scrambling up the rock, he slid over the top and wedged himself between two sheer faces to watch the road. Less than five minutes later, he saw two Texas Rangers ride past. The lawmen never so much as glanced in his direction. Slocum waited a few minutes and started to clamber up— and almost got caught.

Two more Rangers rode behind their partners. Slocum recognized Jeffers immediately. The simple act of staring at the Ranger caused him to turn and look around intently. Slocum flopped down on the rock like a sunning lizard and did not move a muscle.

"You hear anything?" Jeffers asked his partner.

"Just the damn wind blowin'," came the answer. "Why?"

"I dunno. I heard something. Maybe I felt it. Like somebody's walkin' on my grave."

"What you been through, you ought to know the feelin'."

The two rode on, never spotting Slocum. Thinking they were out of earshot, Slocum slid on down the backside of the rock to the sandy spit and then collapsed to the ground. He held out his hands. They shook the slightest amount.

"They're getting to you," Slocum told himself. "What you need is a bottle of whiskey and one of those Mexican señoritas down Sonora way." He touched the money in his pocket, thinking it might have evaporated. After all he had been through since finding that strongbox, losing it might be the best thing that could happen to him. What had seemed like good luck at the time had given him nothing but misery.

He leaned back, pulled down his hat to shade his face, and chuckled. He ought to throw away the money he found and get on back to Bitter Springs and rob the bank. Money he had come by honestly enough gave him trouble. That told him he ought to sample some ill-gotten gains if he wanted to change his luck.

Scraping sounds alerted him that he wasn't alone. His hand crept to his six-shooter as he sat up and looked around. Whatever he had heard wasn't human. He stood and peered down a narrow draw in time to see a rabbit running away from the road as if its life depended on it. Slocum made his way back around the rock and listened hard. Caught on the wind were sounds coming from the direction taken by the Rangers.

". . . damn good thing you saw 'em. That'd been a fight if we crossed them Rangers."

Slocum could not make out the answer, but he didn't have to have much of an imagination to know who it was on the road to Frijole. Cutting their saddle cinches had not slowed Toombs's friends that much. How they had decided this was the way he had headed, he didn't know. More bad luck maybe, or there might be enough of them to split and take each road, some going westward and the rest coming this direction. That was a chilling thought. If they had split in half at Bitter Springs, some going down toward Fort Suddereth and the rest coming up to the fork, that meant they had split again there. Half had gone across the dry lake bed and the rest had headed for Frijole—and there were still at least two of them.

Not once did he think those men were any kind of trackers who had sorted out his hoofprints among all the others and come after him. Or had they? Slocum slid back to where he had tethered his horse and examined the right front hoof. While the shoe was securely in place, he saw that the farrier had nicked it in several places so it would leave a distinctive print. Still, while a tracker as good as Slocum himself might follow the faint marks, he doubted the men decked out in the gray Confederate garrison caps could.

He slid his rifle from its sheath and went back to the top of the rock to watch the road. He wasn't above shooting them both out of the saddle. If they had ridden with Toombs, they were rotten to the core and deserved their fate. They probably had wanted posters following them around Texas.

An idea slowly took form in Slocum's head. He hurried back to his horse and mounted. The going was rough, sliding between rocks and riding parallel to the road. He headed back to the fork and took a few seconds to see that the Texas Rangers had returned to Bitter Springs. Putting his heels to his horse, he galloped a quarter mile until the slower-moving lawmen spotted him. Slocum stayed low in the saddle and immediately swung about and hightailed it in the direction of Frijole.

When he was sure the Rangers were coming after him to see who was so willing to gallop a horse in the Texas heat, he cut off the road and lost himself once more in the jumble of rocks. His mare panted harshly from the exertion, but they were hidden from the road as the Rangers raced past.

It took them only seconds to spot the Confederate-capped men and begin shooting. That told Slocum he had been right.

"Too bad I can't claim the reward," he said, patting his horse.

"Too bad you mighta cost me a pair of good men," came a cold voice. "Like you already cost me the services of Rufus Toombs."

Slocum swung around. He had not heard the man with the sawed-off shotgun approach. He stared down the double barrels of that deadly weapon and knew the man holding it would squeeze the triggers and never think twice.

Slocum knew him all too well.

"Howdy, Jack," Slocum said. "It's been a spell."

"That it has, Slocum," answered Rebel Jack Holtz as he raised the weapon and sighted along the barrels. "And it's gonna be a lot longer till the next time. See you in hell."

7

"Don't go doing anything you will regret, Jack," Slocum said. "You always were a hotheaded son of a bitch who shot first and thought later."

"I've thought this through, Slocum. You killed one of my best men."

"If Toombs was one of your best, you've got a sorry-ass bunch of men riding with you."

Rebel Jack Holtz did not lower his shotgun, but Slocum saw his finger relax on the triggers.

"Why'd you have to go and kill Rufus?"

"Toombs was a back-shooter from way back. I doubt he killed anyone face-to-face in his life. Him and me tangled when we rode with Quantrill."

"I rode with Quantrill, too," Rebel Jack said. "But it was after you got shot."

"Do tell," Slocum said coldly. He didn't doubt that Holtz had ridden with the butchering madman from Ohio. But when Slocum and Holtz had been in the same unit six months before the Lawrence massacre, he had not shown the ruthlessness that Quantrill expected from his men. Slocum and Holtz had been assigned as scouts for one of Nathan Bedford Forest's colonels. They had been run ragged by a Yankee cavalry officer name of Ben Grierson. Slocum had heard that Grierson was commanding the Tenth Cavalry or maybe just Fort Davis, and had swung clear of the fort as a result.

But he and Holtz had gone on more than one mission together, and the result had never been satisfactory. Holtz was more likely to turn tail and run than he was to do an adequate scouting job. Then he'd put the blame on someone else's head for his failure. He had tried to do that once to Slocum and had not liked the result. In spite of this, Slocum and Holtz had gotten along all right. Not friends, not comrades in arms who would die for each other, but there had been a wary truce.

"Toombs and I got to be real pals during our time with Quantrill," Rebel Jack said. "After the war, we came West and recruited some others from the CSA."

"I saw them wearing their garrison caps. That's a mighty foolish thing to do. Why not announce who you are with a brass band and a big parade?"

"You always spoke your mind, Slocum, even if it got you in trouble. I remember that now."

"You never forgot it, Jack. That's one thing about you that's damn near perfect. You never forget."

The outlaw grinned and lowered his shotgun, keeping the stock tucked under his arm and the muzzle pointed in Slocum's direction. With such a weapon, all Holtz had to do was come close. The heavy buckshot spreading out would be certain to strike anything within twenty feet.

"I can't hardly believe it, Slocum. You're payin' me a compliment."

"You would have shot me the instant you laid eyes on me if you'd wanted me dead."

"I might need some help springin' my boys from wherever the Rangers lock 'em up. They've got rewards on their shaggy heads."

"How many in your gang? Got to be a fair number."

"The Rebel Jack Holtz Gang, that's what they call us," the outlaw said.

"I heard. The Rangers back in Sidewinder mentioned you."

"Do tell. Famous. I'm damn famous!"

Slocum did not reply. He waited for more. Holtz didn't disappoint him.

"When I heard the description of the man who had gunned down Toombs, I knew it was you. I thought you were dead. I really did. Everyone in Quantrill's Raiders said so, including Bill Anderson. And who's not going to take him at his word?"

"You reckoned it was me who drilled Toombs, so you came looking for me to reminisce about old times?"

"Something like that. Now that Toombs is lookin' to get himself planted out in a potter's field, I need someone to take his place."

"Filling his boots wouldn't be hard."

"Harder'n you might think, Slocum. He was a special fellow. He knew artillery and explosives."

Slocum looked harder at Holtz. The man was hinting at something, and Slocum wondered why he didn't just spit it out. After all, he was the one holding the shotgun.

"Yup, Toombs was a first-rate artillerist," said Holtz.

"He was a first-rate chucklehead."

"Fer crossin' you, I have to agree. I talked to the barkeep. He said you're quick with that iron of yours, Slocum, real quick." Holtz lifted his shotgun and tapped the barrel. "That's why we're havin' this talk the way we are."

"I thought you wanted to talk me to death. Not sure I wouldn't rather you just pulled both triggers."

Holtz laughed.

"I remember your wit now, Slocum. You have quite a sense of humor, don't you?"

"Yeah, Toombs laughed himself to death."

Holtz lost his smile and tightened his grip on the sawed-off shotgun. Then he spun, the scattergun going to cover two men thrashing their way through the cactus patch behind him.

Slocum went for his own gun and drew it, but hesitated.

Escape was a better option than shooting it out since four men wearing the Rebel garrison caps were now struggling to reach Holtz. All of them had their six-shooters out waving in the air.

Using his knees, Slocum turned his mare, only to find his way out blocked, too. Three more of Holtz's gang had rifles leveled at him. He shrugged and holstered his six-gun. Some hope remained that he could get out of this alive. Holtz could have cut him in half with a double load of buckshot at any time and hadn't. He wanted something, and Slocum thought it might have to do with Rufus Toombs being dead.

"Settle down, boys," Holtz called. "I got things under control."

"He's the one. He kilt Toombs, and he sicced them Rangers onto us."

Hearing this, Slocum had to laugh. These were the men who had passed him on the road and had never known it.

"I'll—" The one doing the complaining lifted his six-shooter and started to fire. Holtz moved like a striking rattler, batting the man's gun hand upward using the barrel of his shotgun so the pistol discharged harmlessly into the air. Slocum never flinched, although he had just come within inches of being cut down.

"What'd you go and do that for, Jack?" The man rubbed his wrist and glared at his boss. "I wanted to kill him for what he done to us, me and Josh. He put them Texas Rangers onto us!"

"He's got the Rangers after him, too," Holtz said. "He only got out of their way. Why didn't you?"

"They come up on us 'fore we even knowed they was there," Josh explained. "It weren't our fault, Jack. Honest."

"Shut up," Holtz said without rancor. "Men!" He shouted now to get the attention of all his gang. "Slocum here's got the Rangers on his ass because he shot one down."

"Twice," Slocum said, but Holtz did not hear him. He was too busy striking a pose and acting like a politician on the stump.

"The Rangers want him somethin' fierce. They want

us, too. That means him and us, we got something in common."

"How many of you hated Toombs?" Slocum asked. He was beginning to enjoy himself now. "Which of you wanted to put a slug into his empty skull?" He saw two of the men smile, just a little. The grins vanished when Holtz shot a dark look at them, then turned his disapproval on Slocum. Slocum did not care at all if Rebel Jack Holtz was pissed at him or not.

"Rufus wasn't the most likable cuss," Holtz said. "That's not what we're talkin' 'bout now. Slocum killin' Toombs isn't what we're talkin' 'bout either."

"Why can't we just drill him, Jack? He killed one of our gang."

"What would you say if I told you Slocum was one of our gang? An important member?" Holtz looked around. Most of the men were confused. A couple were angry. Slocum was just plain curious where Holtz was leading with this.

"Toombs was our explosives expert. Slocum here worked as an officer of artillery. He knows everything there is to know about cannon. Isn't that so, Slocum?"

"I commanded a battery for a while," Slocum admitted. He had learned the rudiments of the science behind aiming and firing, although he and his crew had never been too good. For the most part, in the skirmishes he had been in, accuracy had meant less than getting a large number of cannonballs lobbed onto the battlefield. The CSA had lost all three of the battles where Slocum had fired the cannon. Luckily, he had been transferred to a cavalry unit as a scout and had shone there.

"See, men? We got a replacement for Toombs who fought for the South. What more could we want?" Holtz sounded sure of himself.

"What's going on?" Slocum asked. "Why do you want an artillerist?"

Holtz grinned crookedly.

"That's part of our scheme to make a few dollars."

"A few?" piped up Josh. "You said we'd all be rollin' in the money. Gold and greenbacks and—"

"And don't go shootin' your mouth off," Holtz said coldly.

"Why not? He's either with us or he ain't," said another.

"Reckon they're right, Slocum," Rebel Jack Holtz said. "You with us or against us?"

Looking around and judging his chances at escape as less than zero, Slocum smiled and said, "How can I turn down such a fine offer of rolling in gold and greenbacks?"

"That's the spirit. If more of our officers had felt that way, the Confederacy wouldn'ta lost."

Slocum studied the rapt faces of Holtz's gang, and saw that for them the war was not over and never would be. He had put the loss behind him, along with the repercussions like carpetbagger judges and Reconstruction. As far as Slocum was concerned, the road stretched ahead of him and not behind.

"Josh, you and Sam go do some scoutin'. I know Slocum's better at it than you, but I want to tell him what we're gonna be doing back in Bitter Springs. Keep away from the Texas Rangers."

"Wait," Slocum said. He looked squarely at Josh and asked, "How'd you get away from the Rangers? You bushwhack them?"

"Naw, we got lucky," he said. His partner Sam jabbed him in the ribs with his elbow. "Why'd you do that?"

"We outrun 'em," Sam said.

"You mean you hid and they passed by you. There's no disgrace in that. There's an entire company of Texas Rangers down in Sidewinder. You go killing them and they'll tear the Guadalupe Mountains apart rock by rock hunting for you."

"Like they are for you?" Josh turned to Holtz and said, "You said he was runnin' from them Rangers fer shootin' one. Why won't he be a lightnin' rod for them?"

"They got other things to do, that's why. Slocum here

will keep out of sight. I'll see to that since he's so important. The Rangers will be after Indians and who knows
what all and forget about Slocum."

"I only shot the Ranger," Slocum said, "and didn't kill
him. He's madder'n a wet hen but is still in the saddle. Like
Rebel Jack says, if things heat up with the Apaches, the
Rangers will have more to worry about than a single
Ranger's wounded pride."

"Don't know," Josh said thoughtfully. "Seems that's
more important to a Ranger than his life. You made him
look foolish. That's the kind of thing that will eat away at a
man's gut for years."

Slocum said nothing. That had been true of Rufus
Toombs. For all he knew, it was also true of Ranger Jeffers.
This reinforced his need to leave Texas and the Guadalupe
Mountains far behind him and find more friendly territory.
The only trouble Slocum saw on the horizon was Holtz
wanting to recruit him to join his gang of misfits.

"You hie on out and make sure the way's safe," Holtz
said. "All of you. I'll escort Slocum to the camp myself."

"Is that a good idea, Jack?" asked a bulky man whose
shirt lacked two buttons right at his bulging belly. "What
you say about him bein' on the run and all is fine, but kin
we trust him?"

"He was a captain in the CSA and rode with Quantrill.
What more do you need to know? He's a good man." Holtz
came over and looked up at Slocum. "Isn't that right,
Slocum?"

"Good," Slocum agreed, vowing to clear out as soon as
Holtz turned his back.

"That way," Holtz ordered, motioning with his sawed-
off shotgun. Slocum slowly rode in the direction indicated,
letting his mare avoid the clumps of prickly pear and
ocotillo that had caused others in Holtz's gang such misery
earlier. Behind him came Rebel Jack, humming to himself.
Slocum halted when he saw a horse in an arroyo. Holtz
hurriedly mounted and motioned for Slocum to follow him
up the sandy, dry riverbed.

Keeping a sharp eye out for landmarks, Slocum knew he could backtrack after they reached Holtz's camp. The outlaw weaved about, thinking this confused his trail. For a greenhorn maybe it would, but a six-year-old Apache could have followed it blindfolded. For the Texas Rangers, it would prove no more difficult. Holtz had never ridden too high in Slocum's estimation, and the hour-long ride to the outlaw's camp did nothing to change the view.

"Here we are. Spent a week scouting this out myself."

Slocum rode around the area, noting how close to the edge of a mesa Holtz had camped. All in all, though, it was well selected. He saw no fewer than three ways the Rangers might attack and five that the outlaws could run.

"Do you worry about smoke from cooking fires?"

"Leave it to you to think of something like that, Slocum. Naw, the smoke is whipped about by the updraft from the side of the mesa. If we use nothing but dried wood, we're invisible."

"I was asking because I'm hungry," Slocum said. He dismounted and went to the edge of the mesa. Squinting, he thought he could make out the sheer butte on the east side of Bitter Springs. He was certain he could make out the mesa on the west side. Of the town, though, he could see nothing. It was hidden between the two upthrusts of land, and heat shimmering off the land turned any building into nothing more than a blur.

"Picked this spot special so we could watch the goings-on in Bitter Springs," Holtz said. He handed Slocum a pair of binoculars. Slocum handed them back.

"Seen the town. What's so interesting there? Other than the bank."

Holtz jumped as if Slocum had stuck him with a pin.

"How'd you know?"

"That you are planning on robbing the bank? I took a gander at it myself. That safe is as secure as any I've ever seen. It's sitting on a brick floor. Was Toombs going to blow the safe? I'd want to check closer, but it might take a full box of dynamite to blow off that door."

"That much would destroy whatever's inside the safe," Holtz said.

"Not if it's gold." Slocum remembered the soldiers moving their boxes from the supply wagon into the bank.

"Fort Suddereth stores its payroll there," Holtz said. "You only been in town a day or two—"

"Less," Slocum corrected.

"And you got this all figured out? I knew I was doing the right thing to recruit you."

"You thinking on riding in with that army of yours and forcing the bank president to open his safe for you?" Slocum had thought about that himself, and then had seen the look in Morton Thompson's eyes. The man valued money above all else, and would die a hundred times before opening the safe. Even if he had a family, he would let his wife and children perish before handing over one cent entrusted to the bank.

"Is that what you'd do?"

"Hell, no. And you weren't thinking to do it either."

"Why do you say that?"

"Because you went on and on about Toombs. What sold me to your gang was artillery experience. You planning on stealing a mountain howitzer from Fort Suddereth and using it on the safe?"

"What would you say to a plan like that?"

"Using a cannon is smart," Slocum said, "but you'd have to drag the cannon and caisson from the fort more than ten miles away. There's no way even a shoddily run fort is going to let you do that. From what I saw, Fort Suddereth is run by the book."

"You said it," Holtz exclaimed. "I tried to ride in and look around, and couldn't even get inside that dinky wall of theirs. I talked to the sutler, but he wouldn't give me the time of day. All I could do was find a rise and use my binoculars to study the fort."

"If you're not going to steal a cannon from the cavalry post, what do you have in mind?"

"A Rebel cannon," Holtz said in a husky, almost reverential whisper. "When Sibley invaded New Mexico, he had an artillery battery, and left one cannon here on his way up to lay siege to Fort Craig."

"He went from Mesilla," Slocum said.

"He split his force. The main body of his troops went up the Rio Grande from Mesilla. Another part brought a cannon with them and were going to come up from behind at Fort Craig."

"Why didn't they make it?"

"The troopers deserted," Holtz said, ice in his voice. "The damn cowards deserted, but not before their commander buried the cannon so the Yanks couldn't get it."

"He spiked it?"

"Buried it. The cannon's in perfect condition."

"Let's see it," Slocum said, warming to Holtz's scheme. Then he saw the outlaw's face. "What aren't you telling me?"

"We don't have the cannon, not exactly."

"What exactly do you have?" Slocum asked. He was not sure he wanted to hear the answer. And when Holtz gave it to him, he knew he had been right.

8

Slocum stared at Rebel Jack Holtz, then laughed harshly.

"That's so dumb you must have got it from Toombs."

"No, no," Holtz said. "It was all written down in Hopkins Sibley's reports. I saw them. He was a good general. He won every last fight against the bluebellies in New Mexico."

"He won them all until that son of a bitch Carrington came swooping down from Colorado and destroyed his supply wagons. Sibley left with his tail between his legs."

"Slocum, it is all in his reports. He sent a couple dozen men with the expedition that came through Bitter Springs. They had to abandon their cannon. Rather than let it fall into Yankee hands, they buried it."

"And left a map?" Slocum shook his head. If he had a dollar for every time he had heard about fabulous treasure or lost mines all being put down on a mysterious map, he would have more gold than anything supposedly buried.

"The major in charge of the expedition did. He left a map."

"Let me see it." Slocum stared in amazement as Holtz seemed to shrink and get confused. He looked like a little boy who had been caught doing something naughty. "You don't even have the map?"

"It's in Bitter Springs. Somewhere."

"Somewhere," Slocum said sarcastically, wondering how long a ride it would be across the dry lake bed to El Paso. Making it in three days was out of the question with constant cavalry patrols. If he got lucky, he could reach the border town in less than a week. After all, he had money. He didn't need to get involved in this harebrained scheme of Rebel Jack Holtz's.

"Think of the gold in that bank," Holtz said urgently, seeing his would-be artillerist growing cold to the notion. "Thousands of dollars."

"Split how many ways?" Slocum tried to count the number of men in Holtz's gang. Six? More?

"We'll see at least a thousand apiece. All we got to do is be ready. There's a huge shipment being brought in by the army within two weeks. Not only are they bringin' the payroll for Fort Suddereth, they're moving down a whale of a lot for Fort Concho, too. The Apaches are givin' 'em fits, and they think shipping the gold straight down from the quartermaster at Fort Union is the way to pay for supplies and payroll."

"Then let's rob the train between here and Fort Union. You got enough men."

"No, Slocum, I don't. There's likely to be a company—two!—accompanyin' the gold shipment. Even Quantrill would be hard-pressed to rob a shipment guarded that well."

Again, Slocum heard the echoes of old times he wished to forget. Holtz talked of William Quantrill as if he were the greatest commander ever to serve the South. He had been nothing but a brutal butcher who enjoyed the slaughter and didn't care spit about military victories or goals. Rebel Jack Holtz was no fit leader for a robbery, even in a small town like Bitter Springs, if he held up men like Quantrill as his ideal.

"Then shoot your way in and—"

"The safe, Slocum, the safe! Getting it open's the problem. See how easy everything is if we use the cannon to blow up the bank? The safe will be easy pickin's then."

"No, no way, count me out," Slocum said. Slocum was ready to throw down on Holtz if he tried to lift the scattergun he carried dangling from a strap over his right shoulder. The shotgun rested under his arm where he could swing it up easily, but there was no way in hell he could be as quick getting it into action as Slocum drawing his Colt Navy.

"What'd he say, Jack?"

Slocum looked over his shoulder. The rest of Holtz's gang had finally made their way to the campsite. If he tried to ride out now, he had an army of rifles and pistols to fight through.

"He said he was thinking over going into Bitter Springs to hunt for the map."

The gang fanned out around him and stood, hands on their weapons. If Slocum said anything but that he was in for the robbery, he likely would be tossed over the edge of the cliff and left for the coyotes to pick his bones.

"I wanted to know where to find the map," Slocum said.

"Then you're in?" Holtz slapped Slocum on the back. "That's the John 'Devil Take the Hindmost' Slocum I knew back in the Quantrill days!"

Slocum made his way back into Bitter Springs as cautiously as he could ten days after meeting up with Rebel Jack. With damned near every lawman in the state hunting for him, he had to be careful. He saw that Preacher Dan's wagon had been moved to the back of the lot where it had been parked before, to give easier access from the street for anyone wanting to come listen to his sermons. Slocum saw how the dirt had been kicked up on the lot, and knew there had been a revival meeting here not too long back. Since it was just after sundown, he suspected Preacher Dan had only finished. Mostly, the wagon had been moved because construction on a church had begun while Slocum was out of town.

"I wondered if you'd be back."

Slocum looked behind him. Standing on the front steps of the now-closed bank stood Tessa Whitmore, arms crossed over her ample breasts and looking daggers at him.

"Had business to attend to," he said.

"What do you think Papa's paying you for?"

"I don't rightly know," Slocum said, grinning. "Truth is, I don't remember him offering to pay me anything at all."

"Then there must be some reason you came back."

"There just might be," Slocum said. "Not all pay's in the form of gold."

"Do tell. Whatever else might you be talking about?" Tessa walked over to where he sat astride his mare. He could hardly call it walking, though. She put such emphasis on swaying her backside all around—just for his benefit—that he thought there should be some new word to describe her. Not even "sashaying" fit what she was doing, and all without the aid of a bustle.

"This is a scenic town," Slocum said, dismounting. "How can I pass up the view?"

"You didn't even get the best view," Tessa said.

"Nope, but the banker man did."

"What?" Tessa spun about, staring at the locked bank door. She swung back, her lips thinned to a line. "There wasn't anybody there."

"No," Slocum said, "but I got a much better view of you swinging back and forth." His eyes dipped to her well-filled blouse.

Anger blazed in her eyes for a moment; then she melted and finally laughed.

"I knew there was a reason I liked you, John."

"Only one?" He grinned even more broadly when her eyes dipped to his crotch and then returned.

"There are chores to do," she said. "Papa needs the horse tended to and then . . ."

"Do you need tending to also?"

"After we've done some work," Tessa said. "I need to get some work to the printer."

"Broadsides?"

"And other things," she said mysteriously. For once, she did not want to play word games with him.

"What's the name of the town paper?" Again, he saw how she became furtive, as if she was hiding something. What it might be, Slocum was at a loss to say.

"The *Bitter Springs Gazette*," she said in a tone that ended all discussion of the matter. This suited Slocum just fine. He had some poking around town of his own to do. Let Tessa sweet-talk the editor of the paper for good reviews of her pa's sermons.

"If the horse is over at the livery stables, it's being taken care of," Slocum said. "I need to get my own in for some grain and currying." He patted the grateful mare on her neck. He had ridden quite a few horses in his day, but seldom had he found any with the mare's heart and determination to keep going in the face of thirst and hunger.

"See to it, John," she said. The smile had returned to her ruby lips. "Then perhaps you can see to feeding other hungers."

With that, Tessa swirled her skirts and left him, again treating him to the sight of her rear end waggling about enticingly. He heaved a sigh, then led his horse to the stables. Slocum made certain to peer inside and count the horses already in stalls. If Texas Rangers stayed for the night, he did not want to accidentally run into any of them. The only other horse besides Dan Whitmore's was a broken-down old nag no self-respecting Ranger would ever ride. He felt safe going in and putting his horse into a stall near the front.

"You back? Figgered you might be gone for a day or two, the way you was talkin'," the stable owner said, coming from the tack room. He smelled of saddle soap and carried a worn bridle that no amount of work would ever return to pristine condition. "Didn't know it'd be more'n a week."

"Needed to find out the lay of the land," Slocum said. "Might be you can answer a question for me."

"I'm not so good on some things. Others I know 'bout all there is worth knowing."

"I heard tell that General Sibley sent a small detachment of soldiers up this way when he invaded New Mexico back in '62," Slocum said, watching the man carefully. The way he averted his eyes and partially turned away told Slocum he had hit a nerve.

"Wasn't here then," the stable owner said. "Truth is, I was up in Colorado and my sentiments leaned toward the Federals. But Old Man Jensen over at the pharmacy, he was a tried-and-true Johnny Reb and has spent purty near his whole life in Bitter Springs."

Slocum nodded as if it meant nothing special to him, but he almost ran to the pharmacy when he left the stable. A hoary old man was just turning the sign around in the door showing the business was closed for the day. He peered out nearsightedly at Slocum, then heaved a sigh and opened the door.

"What kin I do you for, mister? I was jist closin' fer the day."

"Let me buy you a drink," Slocum said. "I heard a rumor and a sizable bet is riding on it."

"Do tell," Jensen said, slipping from the pharmacy and closing the door behind him. He patted his pockets for the key, didn't find it, and shrugged. He smiled at Slocum and said, "Ain't got nuthin' in there worth stealin'. The secret to my medicine's in the mixin's, not the fixin's. Now what's this bet all about?"

They walked slowly toward the nearest saloon. Slocum wanted to rush, but the old man's step was short and hesitant and not to be hurried.

"It's all about how General Sibley came through Bitter Springs back in '62 on his way to Fort Craig."

"Ain't so. If you took that side o' the bet, you jist lost. Sibley never came here," Jensen said with some satisfaction at thinking he was giving Slocum information he lacked. Slocum only wanted to check that the old man's memory was accurate. So far, it appeared to be.

They went into the saloon and settled down. The barkeep set a half-full bottle of whiskey in front of Jensen without being asked. Slocum paid for it, to the barkeep's surprise.

"I usually drink alone," Jensen said. "These young bucks don't want to hear no tall tales about my life." He knocked back a quick shot, made a face, then said, "This here whiskey's better medicine than anything I brew up. Takes the ache away, at least till it chews through my stomach."

"So General Sibley only sent a small detachment?" Slocum prodded.

"The Sibley Brigade went right up the Rio Grande. The Jornado del Muerto. Most folks don't know it, but Sibley was General Canby's brother-in-law. The thought of her husband facin' her brother mighta put Miz Sibley into a fit, but from what I hear, she was a good military wife and kept her thoughts to herself. Might have been, she wanted her husband to do somethin' right for once in his life. And invadin' New Mexico and takin' it for the South would have been it. He thought to have some artillery sneak up behind the damn bluebellies at Fort Craig right outside Socorro. Didn't work out right fer him, but then not much did."

"What happened? Here in Bitter Springs?"

Jensen smiled broadly.

"Me and a couple others tried to warn the fools away, but they came right on into town. Troopers from Fort Union way up close to Las Vegas were scoutin'. Weren't many of 'em. Not more than a dozen, but they was more'n a match for the Rebs. Bad training, overconfident, not a decent officer with 'em—all them was true. Mostly, I think it was outright cowardice. None of them soldiers had ever been fired at in battle, and the bluebellies was all veterans of fightin' Indians. Face a Comanche and live, ain't no human bein' ever gonna scare you again." Jensen worked some more on the whiskey. Another shot steadied his hand and loosened his tongue even more.

"The Rebs tried to run. The only decent thing they done was try to save their two cannons."

"They had two?"

"They buried 'em."

"Where?" Slocum tried not to sound too excited. It hardly seemed possible, but Rebel Jack's scheme might have a chance of working if he could find those cannons.

"Now that is a matter of some conjecture. I heard some tales of them draggin' the guns with them as they hightailed it back down to San Angelo. Ain't true. I saw them retreatin', and they didn't have a caisson or cannon with 'em."

"You have any idea where they buried the guns?"

"One story I heard was that a sergeant made a map and hid it, thinking Sibley would come through eventually and retrieve the guns. Reckon that might be so, but where'd a sergeant hide a map that a general could find?"

"Where do you think?"

"Can't say I think much of it at all," Jensen said. "Drink up, son. You paid for the bottle. You oughta git some enjoyment out of the whiskey."

Slocum obliged, but found his thirst had changed from whiskey to information.

"Nobody ever found the map?"

"Don't reckon they'd have to. Who'd want a cannon anyway?"

"If it had been buried, it wouldn't be much use," Slocum opined.

"You ain't from around here, are you? Bury somethin' in this desert sand and it don't rust, it don't corrode, it stays jist like you put it down, fer a long, long time."

Slocum's hopes soared again.

"Nope, don't need a map since I know what happened to the cannon," said Jensen. "It's the only explanation."

"What is?"

"They buried the cannons, all right, but not with shovels. They prob'ly didn't have time fer that. No, sir, I think they hid them guns in a mine shaft. There's a passel of 'em in the hills just outside town. A piece of cake for even green soldiers to wheel their guns in, then ride off."

"I saw some petered-out mines," Slocum said. "They

looked recent, though. Any mine they put their cannon into would have to be at least fifteen years abandoned."

"Yup, some tin miners came through not five years back and dug like prairie dogs in the hills. Didn't find a damn thing, though they did go west and found some tin in the Franklin Mountains. Earlier miners was huntin' fer silver."

"Which claims?"

"You lookin' to jump a claim or winnin' a bet?" Jensen looked at Slocum suspiciously. The whiskey was taking the edge off his garrulousness rather than encouraging it. Slocum guessed Jensen turned into a mean drunk, which might be one reason nobody in town liked to drink with him.

"Betting's more fun, and you're not as likely to get shot at," Slocum answered.

"Ain't never been that way that I kin see."

"The mountains east of Bitter Springs?"

"Played out early on. Right after the silver rush in '60."

"Thanks," Slocum said. He left with Jensen beginning to rant about young whippersnappers not having any courtesy left in their bones these days.

Stepping out into the cold desert night invigorated him, but Slocum knew he had to wait for morning and light to hunt for the mine where Sibley's soldiers had hidden not one but two cannons.

9

Slocum spent a restless night, coming awake more than once at the slightest of sounds. When he did drift off, his dreams were haunted by Rebel Jack Holtz and his gang, the pharmacist Jensen, and facing artillery fired at him by CSA soldiers. The more he tried to run or cry out that he was a friend, the more they came after him.

When he finally stirred just before sunrise, he was less rested than if he had stayed awake all night. He sat up and brushed himself off. His mare slept in the next stall. Slocum knew he should have hunted for Tessa Whitmore the night before. Spending the night with her would have been far more pleasant, not to mention that he could have done so lying beside her in a hotel bed. But he had left the saloon, and Jensen muttering at him, too tired to go on. More than that, Slocum wanted an early start. If he hung around Bitter Springs long enough for Tessa and her pa to find him, they would keep him busy with make-work.

He had a Rebel cannon to find.

He saddled and rode the mare from town just as the sun peeked above the mountain peak to the east of town. The sheer face of rock was still hidden in shadow by the time he found a road leading into the hills and took it. Slocum studied the ground, and saw no evidence that any heavy wagons had come this way within the past few weeks. For all he knew, nothing might have rolled this way in years. The ruts in the road were sunbaked and harder than rock. While the desert vegetation would overgrow any patch of ground sooner or later, he thought this road was more likely too alkaline for plants to grow rather than being well traveled.

Turning his face upward, he studied the sides of the mountains reaching as far ahead as he could see. The canyon bottom where the road took him had once acted as the main thoroughfare for miners. From the ancient look of the gaping mouths of the mines dotting the mountainsides, no one had worked here for maybe seventeen years. That was about when a Rebel force would have hidden their artillery before running back to Texas.

Slocum pursed his lips as he considered why a Confederate detachment would have used this canyon and these mines for their hiding place. He kept riding until almost noon before he convinced himself of the reason. The road led to a branching canyon that opened southward. Slocum guessed it was somewhere to the east of Sidewinder. From there, it was a quick trip into the West Texas desert.

He turned back, and this time studied the lowest mines to find the most likely ones where cannons would be stashed. Too high up on the mountain meant effort—and time—for fleeing soldiers. They'd had only a short time to evade the Federals from Fort Union.

"There," Slocum said, eyeing a mine low on the mountain and easily reached from the canyon floor. There were others closer to the canyon floor, but crossing arroyos or deep ravines made them less accessible. Slocum knew it was a long shot that he had found the proper mine after only a few hours of hunting, but everything Jensen had told him fit well with what he knew of Confederate tactics and the lay of the land. The other mines might not have been as isolated back in the day, but Slocum's gut told him this mine was the place to start his search.

He urged his mare up the rocky path to the mine opening, and looked around for any trace that the mine had operated recently. He dismounted and poked through a pile of discarded equipment just outside the mouth of the mine. He found a small book and sat down, his back against a wood mine support, and flipped through the pages.

As he let the pages flip freely, a slip of paper fell out. He peered at it. The ink had faded with time, but he finally caught the sunlight against the page and saw he held a receipt for Giant blasting powder dated in 1861. Slocum closed the book and let it fall open to the front page. The printing date was 1858. If Sibley had sent his detachment in '62, this mine had been scrabbled out of the rocky mountainside the year before.

It would not have taken a year to play out. From all Slocum had heard, silver had never been found in any abundance in the Guadalupe Mountains, and tin, which prospectors had found just north of El Paso eighty-five miles to the west, was nonexistent here.

He tucked the receipt back in the pages of the book and tossed it aside. It almost disintegrated from this mistreatment after so many years of sun and wind and cold. Slocum walked back and forth in front of the mine opening, studying the ground. He finally reached down, picked up a rusty piece of iron, and held it up to get a better look at it in the sunlight. He frowned as he turned it over and over in his hand.

It might have been the sighting adjustment bracket off a cannon. Or it might have been a bracket used for something else by a miner scrounging for any hunk of metal he could find. Slocum tossed it back on the ground and stared into the dark shaft. To go inside would be dangerous. The timbers supporting the roof were rotted, and such holes in the ground were natural dens to animals both small and large. Slocum did not remember any stories of bears in these mountains, but there were cougars and coyotes who would find such a mine a natural home.

Slocum checked his six-shooter in case he ran afoul of rattlers, then looked at the ledges just inside the mouth for miners' candles. Not finding any, he spent the next twenty minutes finding dried brush and rags to tie onto a long pole to use as a torch. He lit the torch and held it at arm's length as it flared. Some of the heavy smoke might pose a problem inside the mine, but Slocum doubted there would be any need to go more than a dozen yards inside. If the artillerists had no reason to drag their cannon higher up, they would not bother putting the cannon more than a few yards deep in the mine.

He thrust the torch into the mine and looked for telltale signs the cannon had been pushed inside. Scratches on the rocky walls, deeper cuts on the floor, anything. What he saw might have been the result of clumsy mining rather than a cannon being dragged inside.

Still, Slocum wanted to check deeper inside just to be sure he did not miss anything. After all, it had been seventeen years since the Rebs would have hidden the cannon. He bent down as he went farther into the dark mine. When he had gone ten yards, he knew there were no cannons here. With a sense of disappointment that a good idea had not panned out, Slocum turned to leave. He saw the bright rectangle of the mouth of the mine ahead as the torch sputtered fitfully and finally burned out. As he started to retrace his steps, his boot heel caught between two rocks on the floor, causing him to stumble and fall.

He let out a loud cry of surprise and then hit the mine floor hard. Coughing at the dust, he pushed to his hands and knees, then heard the ominous creaking noise over his head. Slocum looked up and could see nothing in the shadowy roof, but he knew the sound. He had worked in mines and feared only two things: gas and breaking timbers.

The decayed wood in this old mine was giving way.

Slocum dug in his toes and tried to sprint out, but whatever had caught his boot before still hung on. He flopped back onto his face as the roof caved in. Hands going over his head to protect himself, he felt the weight of rocks crashing down on top of him. For what seemed an eternity, the cave-in continued. Then there was nothing. No sound, no light, nothing but the heavy throbbing of his heart trying to explode from his chest.

Heaving with all his might, he got the stones off that had fallen on top of him. He gagged on the thick dust. Using his bandanna over his nose and mouth helped. He would have been better able to filter the thick dust if he had soaked the cloth in water, but he had no water. No light. No air.

At this thought, Slocum's lungs began to strain.

"Stop it," he said loudly. The echo in the mine was muted, telling him the crash of timber and rock had momentarily deafened him, but his hearing was returning slowly. More than this, the words helped him regain his senses. Panic now would kill him.

The lack of light confused him. He knew which direction he had been walking when he had stumbled, but the best he could guess was that the solid wall of rock had fallen between him and safety. Never had he wanted the hot Texas sun burning his face more. After tying his bandanna into place, he fumbled in his vest pocket until he found his tin of lucifers. A quick strike got a match lit to reveal the horror of his situation.

Buried alive.

This was probably his worst nightmare. He turned slowly, keeping the lucifer burning as long as he could. When it singed his fingers, he dropped it. The wood sputtered a second or two longer on the floor and then winked out. Slocum had his bearings now, though. He pressed his hands against the rock wall and shoved, hoping to dislodge a few rocks and dig a small tunnel to the outside. Air and light would go a long way toward restoring his composure.

After pulling down rocks for what seemed an eternity, Slocum was no closer to digging through the rockfall than before he'd started. He lit a second lucifer to convince himself he had not gotten turned around and tried to claw his way through a side wall. If anything, he would have had better luck trying that. The plug of rock blocking his way out might extend for yards. He was lucky that he had stumbled when he did. If he had gone another few feet, the worst of the rockfall would have crushed him like a bug.

"Lucky, yeah, that's me," he muttered. He sat and rested, gathering his strength and trying to come up with a way out of the mine.

Thoughts flashing to the cannon he sought, a crazy plan formed. Find the cannon, load it, and blow his way through the rock. Even as the idea blossomed, it wilted. It was crazy. The explosion in such a cramped space would kill him, even if he found gunpowder, shot, and a cannon that would not blow up.

"Tools," he decided. They were the only way he was going to escape. Would a miner more than seventeen years ago have left a pick behind? A length of rod Slocum could use as a lever to pry stones loose? Anything?

"It's only money," he said, finding the greenbacks wadded up in his shirt pocket. He folded several together, spit on them, and then lit the money. By wetting the bills, he kept them from burning too fast. Slocum used the light cast by the burning scrip to hurry deeper into the mine in his hunt for tools. As the money burned down, he took out more bills and let the first ignite the next.

Deeper and deeper he went into the mine. The flickering light of burning ten-dollar bills showed where a miner had chipped away at the walls, hunting for precious metal. Not even fool's gold reflected back as Slocum plunged deeper into the side of the mountain. An unexpected bend in the mine forced him to angle away and downward. Still no tools. The greenbacks had begun to turn to ash in his fingers when he saw it.

He let out a yelp of triumph and lunged forward as the last of the bills he held flickered out. His fingers closed around a crowbar left behind by the last miner. More than this, he had spotted a few kegs of blasting powder. Eager now, he took out his tin of lucifers and felt inside for the matches.

Slocum cried out again, this time in anger. He had one match left. One.

Unable to see in the dark, Slocum felt around like a blind man, fingers seeking to make sense of what they touched. He found three small kegs of black powder. Using his crowbar to pry the end off one, Slocum dipped his finger into the powder inside and sniffed. It was blasting powder, but was it still good after so many years? If it had been left here more recently, Slocum knew he had a better chance of it igniting properly.

But there was no way to test it first, not with only one match.

Again, he sat in the dark and stewed. His mind turned over one scheme after another until only one came to him. He heaved a deep breath, stood, and picked up a keg of powder. Retracing his steps, he found the rockfall again by walking into it. He left the keg, counted steps back, and retrieved the other two.

Then he spent what had to run into hours using the crowbar to pull down rock from the barrier between him and daylight to make a cavity suitable for holding two kegs of powder. He had done some blasting in his day, and knew the more rock he placed on the kegs, the more powerful the explosion would be in the direction he wanted.

When he finished placing the two kegs, he used the contents of the one he had opened to make a fuse running back down the mine. He had gone ten paces when he ran out. The trail of gunpowder leading to the kegs buried in rock would act as a crude fuse. The resulting explosion would blast through the rock and open the mine again.

If the gunpowder was still good. If the blast didn't bring down more rock on his head. If he could even ignite the powder fuse.

"To hell with it," he said. "I can 'if' myself to death faster than I can blow myself up."

He fumbled about and found the end of the powder fuse, then reached into his pocket and pulled out his last lucifer. Slocum took a deep breath, then struck the match.

It did not light.

10

Slocum held down his initial panic and tried the lucifer again. Still no familiar flame at the end of the wood stick. He tried a third time and broke the matchstick. He heard the pieces go skittering away in the darkness, but finding them would be impossible. The mine floor was covered with gravel and inch-deep dust in places.

He sat down and collected his thoughts. He had been in worse spots before.

"Steel, flint, spark," he said, reaching down to pick up the crowbar. He swung it against the wall and sent the metal bar skittering along the face. No sparks. He tried other places, and got no satisfactory results. The iron was too corroded. Even if he used his knife, he doubted he could get a spark out of the rock. Everywhere he tried, the rock of the walls and floor was too soft to produce a spark good enough to ignite the powder. If the gunpowder would even catch fire.

Slocum sat and thought some more, and finally he moaned as he realized he had the perfect way of setting fire to the fuse. He drew his six-shooter and cocked it. The Colt Navy felt familiar in his hand, and was a trusted companion that had gotten him out of worse predicaments than this.

Once more, he felt around until he found the last of the gunpowder.

"Let's see if my luck's changed," he said, placing the muzzle at the end of the gunpowder trail. He pointed the barrel along the fuse, knowing the muzzle flash would be at least a foot long. This gave him a better chance of setting off his fuse. He closed his eyes and pulled the trigger.

The report was deafening in the closed space. He hoped it would not end up being his tomb. Slocum opened his eyes and saw the hissing, sizzling trail moving away from him toward the kegs of powder buried under his carefully placed rocks. Getting to his feet, he ran for all he was worth, banging his head repeatedly on the low ceiling. He slipped and skidded on his butt down the slope to where the gunpowder had been cached. He came to a halt as the explosion sent a crushing fist down the tunnel and again robbed him of hearing.

In shock and unable to stand for several seconds, Slocum lay in the rubble caused by the new blast. When he struggled to his feet, he knew this was the moment of decision. He still had bullets left. He might have to use one on himself rather than die of suffocation or thirst in the utter darkness of the mine.

He scrambled up the slope to the main shaft and cried out with relief. A tiny shaft of light angled toward him, causing him to squint. The sunlight came through a tiny hole at the top of the rockfall and was filtered by the choking cloud of dust kicked up by the explosion, but he had fresh air coming in—and a way out.

Slocum picked up the rusty crowbar and ran to the pile of rocks. Where there had been big rocks, now there were fist-sized hunks and smaller. The blasting powder had done its work well. Applying the crowbar to the top of the pile, he levered out one rock after another, until there was room enough for him to get his head and shoulders into the small shaft he had first blasted and then cleared out by dint of hard work.

Taking off his six-shooter, he shoved himself into the

tiny passage and began wiggling like a snake. Sharp-edged rocks cut into him, but he did not mind. Every second brought him closer to the canyon and escape from a premature burial. When he finally flopped out, he simply lay in the light, letting the heat soak into his aching bones. Then he knew what had to be done. He got back up to his small crawl space and wormed his way halfway through until he could grab his gun belt. Backing up proved harder than he thought, and he got caught a couple times. He had mostly ripped away his vest and part of his shirt by the time he tumbled back out. But he had his six-gun, and wasted no time strapping it back on.

He had defied death and was ready to whip his weight in wildcats.

He stepped into the bright light, and was amazed to find the sun only a little past zenith. He thought he had been trapped in the mine for hours. He took out his pocket watch and stared at it. Then he shook it, turned the stem a couple times to be sure it was wound and ticking, and replaced it in his watch pocket.

"I'll be damned," Slocum said. "Less than two hours. That's all I was in there. I know what hell is going to be like now."

He dusted himself off, and had started to fetch his mare when he saw something that stopped him in his tracks. A lariat stretched out on the ground. It had been looped around a support for the mine roof and then tugged on hard enough to pull the beam free. Slocum picked the rope up and ran his fingers along it. This was a brand-new rope, and it had not been here when he had gone into the mine.

His six-shooter came out of its holster and into his hand as he surveyed the terrain, hunting for whoever had tried to kill him. He saw nothing but the greasewood and mesquite bending gracefully in a rising afternoon wind. He closed his eyes and listened. Wind. Soft wind moving through vegetation and nothing more. Then, he realized whoever had pulled the support from the mine to kill him had a couple hours' head start.

Slocum slowly looped the rope and carried it downhill to where his mare strained and jerked on her bridle. He soothed the frightened horse. The succession of loud noises had spooked her, but Slocum felt the need to get on the trail right away.

The trail of the son of a bitch who had tried to kill him.

He rode straight to the canyon floor and cast an expert eye on the road he had followed in. His tracks were still visible in the hard ground. Another set, coming in and departing, had been added after his. That the hoofprints did not go past where Slocum had turned to go into the mine told him he had been followed. Whoever had ridden behind him had had only one thing in mind.

Kill John Slocum.

He touched the ebony butt of his Colt Navy and vowed the next shot would be through a cowardly heart. Slocum didn't hold much with gunfighting, but it was more honest than bushwhacking a man or burying him alive in an old mine. He put his heels to the mare's flanks and trotted along the road. There wouldn't be any need to find new prints until he reached the mouth of the canyon. From this road, there was nowhere to go but out.

When he reached the main road running into Bitter Springs, Slocum had to do some fancy tracking. The would-be killer had ridden away from town. As Slocum followed, an idea formed as to the identity of the man. Slocum couldn't put a name to him, but he knew where to find him.

When the tracks crossed solid rock, not even an Apache could follow. Slocum did not have to. He rode directly for Rebel Jack's camp on the mesa. By an hour past sundown, he was a quarter mile away. Leaving his mare tethered, Slocum took the rope used to pull down the support beam and went the rest of the way up the narrow trail on foot. Somehow, in spite of it being a moonless night, his vision was acute and the starlight almost too brilliant for him. That was the difference between being trapped to die in a mine and being free under the wide-open sky.

Rebel Jack either had not posted a sentry, or the man had decided to catch a few winks instead of standing guard. It hardly mattered to Slocum which it was. He was going into camp one way or the other—but he preferred to do it without anyone seeing him.

He came to the rope corral where the outlaws' horses were tied. They made small annoyed sounds as he drifted through the remuda. He found one with thorns in its legs and more than a few cuts showing it had been ridden earlier and the owner had not bothered tending his animal. Finding the saddle and gear belonging to the horse's owner was equally simple. The only one without a lariat had to be the right one.

Moving like a shadow, Slocum slipped closer to camp. Two fires blazed, one for cooking and the other to keep the men warm. He settled down a few yards away unnoticed. At first, he heard only the usual night sounds. Then, he began catching snippets of conversation. One seemed to boom loudly in his head.

"Yup, I got even with him fer killin' my cousin."

"You never said Toombs and you was related. How come?"

"Would you admit bein' cousin to a crazy man like Rufus? I didn't say nuthin', so neither did he. But he was blood."

"Blood," agreed the second man. "You got to stand up for blood kin, no matter what." There was a long pause, then: "You say you faced down Slocum? You killed him fair and square, Josh?"

"I certainly did." The sound of a pistol sliding across leather came to Slocum's ears. He was going for his own six-shooter when he checked the motion. He caught a glint in the firelight of a man holding up a gun. Slocum hadn't been spotted. Josh was only showing his partner how he had gotten the drop on Slocum and then gunned him down.

"He's fast. That's what all of 'em in town said. And Rebel Jack said so, too. How'd you ever outdraw him?"

"I'm fast," Josh boasted. "I'm faster—I'm faster than Slocum ever was." He laughed.

"You gonna tell Jack? I think he was takin' a shine to Slocum. And we got to find ourselves somebody else to fire that cannon if we're gonna open up the bank like a tin of sardines."

"I kin fire the cannon, once we find it."

"Jack thought Slocum was our best chance of findin' it. Ain't none of us got any notion a'tall where the map is."

"He didn't know either," Josh said. "He was wanderin' all over that canyon, lost as a little lamb. Then I butchered him like a goat!"

"Still, Josh, you're takin' a big risk of offendin' Jack."

"I ain't afraid of him," Josh declared. Slocum heard the slight quaver in the man's boast. He was afraid of Rebel Jack Holtz. That meant he didn't have the sense God gave a goose.

He should have been afraid of John Slocum.

Slocum judged where the campfire was in relation to the sheer drop-off. He circled, found a sturdy rock, and secured the end. He played out the rest of the rope, got a loop formed, and then began swinging it over his head. Slocum had worked enough herds to be expert in roping. For a moment, he felt a pang that he had left the Double Cross Ranch and Mr. Benton, but there was no way the ranch owner could have kept his herd going after so many disasters had befallen him.

Slocum started walking toward the campfire, whirling the rope above his head. Another disaster was about to befall one of Rebel Jack's henchmen.

He got all the way up to the circle of light cast by the fire before the men noticed. Slocum knew they might be half-drunk, or maybe they were just too confident the Rangers and other lawmen would never find them perched on the top of this mesa.

"Wha—" Josh jumped to his feet and stared. When he recognized Slocum, he blanched. Then he went for his gun. He was far too late. Slocum let fly with the lariat. The loop dropped neatly around the man's upper arms. A hard yank cinched the rope down so tight, Josh could not move his arms, much less draw his pistol.

"You shouldn't have used this rope to pull out the support in the mine," Slocum said. "I reckon I'll have to show you how the rope ought to be used."

"Slocum, wait, you son of a bitch!" Josh struggled to get free, but Slocum was already dragging him from the fire. When the outlaw went to his knees, Slocum pulled harder and pulled him through the dirt. "You can't get away with this, Slocum!"

"Like you thought you could get away with burying me alive in that mine?" Slocum dug his heels in and yanked with all his strength. Josh went sliding, hit a slope, and then tumbled over the side of the mesa.

His agonized shrieks cut through the night like the howl of a banshee.

"Good Lord, man, you done throwed him over the cliff." Josh's partner, Sam, ran to the edge and looked over. "He's just danglin' down there. That rope's cuttin' into his arms."

"If he struggles too much, he'll fall. How far do you think it is to the bottom of the cliff?"

"More'n a hundred feet, I'd say." Sam turned to his friend and turned back, not sure what he ought to do.

By this time, the rest of the Holtz gang had come running, including Rebel Jack himself.

"What the hell's goin' on, Slocum?"

"I was just getting rid of some garbage," Slocum said. The rope bounced all over the edge of the cliff as Josh continued to swing about and fight to get free.

"Jack, he threw Josh over the side. That's him screamin' bloody murder down there." Sam chanced another look over the side of the cliff.

"Bloody murder," Slocum said coldly. "That's what he tried to do to me. He had his chance."

"What are you going to do, Slocum?" Holtz demanded. "I need all the men . . ." His voice trailed off as Slocum drew his six-shooter.

Slocum aimed and fired. The first slug tore through half the rope holding Josh.

"Damn," Slocum said. "Missed. Must be I'm still shook up from being buried in that mine most of the afternoon." He fired again. This round cut through the remaining strands of the rope.

Josh's frightened cries could be heard all the way down to the bottom of the cliff. The wet smashing noise sounded like a pumpkin had been dropped from the top of the mesa.

"Must have hit his head. I hope the rest of that snake's dead. I'd hate to have to go down there to finish the job," Slocum said. He held his six-gun easily, looking around the circle of men staring at him aghast. Sam kept his hands far from his six-shooter, to be certain Slocum did not decide to plug him and add to what might become a pile of corpses at the bottom of the cliff.

"You let him fall," one said.

"He shouldn't have left his rope behind. It must have frayed when he pulled that support out."

"Josh was Toombs's cousin, Jack," said Sam. "I never knowed that. Did you?"

"His cousin? That's the dumbest thing I ever heard," Rebel Jack said. "Josh was from New Jersey. Toombs was a Texican born and bred. They weren't related."

"But he said—"

Slocum lowered the hammer on his six-shooter with a metallic click that silenced the man. Josh had lied to give himself a reason to kill Slocum and then brag on it. There might have been other reasons, but Slocum had never seen Josh before. That meant the dead man was only out to kill to enhance his standing in the Holtz gang.

"He fell the whole danged way," said another of the gang, tentatively looking over the edge of the cliff. He turned and stared at Slocum with a mixture of fear and admiration in his eyes. "Josh was a lyin' sidewinder who never did anything honest in his life."

"He woulda double-crossed us all," said another. "I say

that Slocum here just kept us all from gettin' killed in our sleep!"

"Looks like you done us all a favor, Slocum," said Holtz. He slapped Slocum on the shoulder, then grinned insincerely. "Yes, sir, you did us a good deed gettin' rid of a mudererin' son of a bitch in our midst."

Slocum said nothing. They were all mudering sons of bitches.

Holtz looked around, then steered Slocum away from the edge of the cliff and to the spot near the fire where Josh and his partner had been only a few minutes earlier.

"Set yourself down. I need to ask you some questions."

"I didn't find the cannon," Slocum said flat out. "If there's a map, I'm not sure where to find it either."

"Where'd you look?"

Slocum was slow in replying. Rebel Jack was more interested in the cannon than he was in the death of one of his henchmen. From all Slocum could tell, Josh had been Holtz's right-hand man. The outlaw leader's easy acceptance of Slocum killing him revealed more about Holtz than anyone needed to know. He would turn his loyalty on its ear if it suited him. Nobody in his gang was indispensable—except Rebel Jack Holtz himself.

"If the army retreated, they would have gone down the canyon leading eventually to Sidewinder. From there, they could escape into the desert since Fort Suddereth hadn't been built yet. No Federal force would have followed. But the mines in that canyon are all played out."

"Perfect place to hide a cannon," Holtz interrupted.

"I thought so, but I had plenty of time to reconsider," Slocum said. "Somebody would have found the cannon in the past seventeen years. I didn't find a whole lot of evidence, but I know prospectors. More than a few of them have rummaged around in those mines, hunting for usable equipment or even color missed by earlier miners. They would have come on the cannon."

"What would a prospector want with a cannon? They'da left it."

"People in Bitter Springs would have heard about it. I followed the best lead I could from a crotchety old man at the pharmacy." Slocum fell silent.

"The map. I know there's a map," insisted Holtz. "Find it and we got ourselves a cannon!"

"Where do I look for the map?" Slocum asked. The only answer he got was a shake of Holtz's head. The outlaw leader had no idea.

Slocum was plumb out of ideas, too.

But that bank with its tempting gold was a lure he wasn't going to deny.

11

Slocum was reluctant to ride back into Bitter Springs, but he felt he had reached a point where he had nothing to lose. The sight of the bank made his mouth water. Before, it had been a fantasy robbing the bank. Now, it was something more. The money he had found in the strongbox out on the desert was all gone up in smoke. He looked down at his right thumb and index finger. The skin was still blistered where he had held the money as he burned it to light his way through the collapsed mine. It might have been money well spent— burned up—since it had kept him alive. The only regret he had was the waste.

He could have bought more than that señorita and bottle of pulque down in Mexico. A string of horses, a few cattle, he could have become a landowner. The idea of constantly drifting wore down on him at times, as it did now. He had lawmen of all kinds after him, as well as the cavalry. He had thrown in with Rebel Jack Holtz, and didn't trust the man enough to even turn his back on him. His life was one giant balancing act, as if he stood on a rope stretched between two high peaks. The slightest mistake and he would tumble to his death.

The money could have given him time to settle down and rest a mite. It would have given him choices.

Slocum snorted as he swung his leg over the saddle and dropped to the ground. It would never happen. If he had a small spread with a few head of cattle, he would be bored in a month and gone in two. Danger was a part of his life— any life. For him, it gave definition, and he appreciated the things it brought to him.

He smiled when he saw Tessa Whitmore coming across the street in his direction.

"Where have you been?" she asked without so much as a "Hello, how are you?"

"Been out roaming around the countryside. This is good country. Might settle down here." He almost laughed as her blue eyes went wide in horror. Tessa covered her shock well and waved her hand about as if shooing away flies— or bad ideas.

"Nonsense, John. You're helping Papa. There is a huge project under way, and he needs all the trustworthy help he can get."

"I see he's moved the wagon and done some digging. What's that about?" Across from the bank, where Preacher Dan had had his wagon before, was now a thriving construction site. Half a dozen men swung hammers and worked on building the church. There had been a fair amount of digging and dirt had been piled up head-high all around, more than Slocum remembered from his examination a couple days earlier.

"A new church takes a considerable amount of hard work to construct," Tessa said. "Papa likes Bitter Springs so much he decided to build a ministry here."

"Do tell," Slocum said. "That going to be your church? Behind all the piles of dirt?"

"Oh, yes," Tessa said with glee, ignoring his implied question about the dirt. "It is going to be about perfect. The foundation is in and helpers are working on the walls. In only a day or two the roof will be set into place, though the actual time to completing the project might amount to weeks."

"Why's that?"

She looked at him sharply, then relaxed as if she understood things he had no idea about.

"There's another church," she said.

"Saw it at the other end of town as I rode around," Slocum said. "So?"

"The pastor is adamant about keeping Papa from building this church. He has preached against us and is trying to turn his flock into vigilantes."

"Vigilantes?"

"He hasn't quite come out and advocated stoning—or burning down our church—but he is perilously close."

"That's not a Christian thing to do," Slocum observed. Tessa was less outraged at this than she was amused. He wondered why. "Something must have put a burr under his saddle."

"It's because of the way Papa raises money, I suspect. Pastor Gantt does not mix commerce with Gospel."

Slocum had to laugh. He suspected Preacher Dan sold as much snake oil as he did salvation. Both could line his pockets well, but the combination added a few extra dollars to the donation bucket not available to Gantt.

"The pastor is quite serious, John. I fear there might be real trouble."

"You want me to guard the church at night?" Slocum's eyes narrowed at the horrified expression on Tessa's face. She shook her head vehemently.

"That won't be necessary, not at all. I'm sure Pastor Gantt is, at heart, a gracious and peaceable man." She nervously smoothed her skirts and flashed him an insincere smile. "If you will excuse me, I need to go to City Hall and look through some records."

"What are you hunting for?" Slocum asked. He wondered if he could ask Tessa to look for the map showing the location of the hidden cannon, if there even was a map—or a cannon. From her businesslike manner, he doubted she would be willing to take the time for his pursuit. He would have to do the searching himself, and he preferred to ask around. People provided easier access to information than a pile of dusty old record books.

Besides, it gave him the chance to drink a whiskey or two.

"You should find Papa and let him know you've finally returned. I am sure there is plenty he can have you do."

Slocum started to tell her he wasn't inclined to work for Preacher Dan, and then remembered how he had burned through his entire poke in the mine. He had a few coins left from his Double Cross pay jingling in his pocket, but not enough to get by on for very long. A job with the preacher would not pay much, but it would be better than no job at all. More than this, it gave him a reason to be around Tessa. For all her brusqueness right now, he had seen her fiery side and liked it. As soon as she found what she looked for in the town records and was no longer focused on that chore, he suspected he would not have to worry about where he was going to sleep at night.

"Where can I find him?" Slocum asked.

Tessa looked around, as if she expected to see her father behind her; then she pointed.

"Down the street at the general mercantile. He was buying tools for use on the church. It is going to be so hard to build, you know."

Slocum wondered why. All Preacher Dan needed were four walls and a roof, and he had done fine without them before. He had not lacked for a crowd when he stood on the back of his wagon to preach his sermons and sell his elixirs. From the industry of the men at work on the church, it was mostly done, except for the roof and finishing off the interior.

"I'll see what needs to be done. I was a fair carpenter once upon a time."

"Were you now?" Tessa said, the sparkle coming to her eyes. She smiled her wicked smile and added in a whisper, "I'd love to see what we could build together, you hammering and me getting nailed."

With that she was off, swaying seductively just for his benefit. Slocum shook his head. He could not quite figure her out. Rather than spending more time trying, he set out for the general store, keeping a sharp watch out for any Texas Rangers. He had not seen a town marshal. Bitter Springs probably did not need one with Fort Suddereth so close by and the Texas Rangers company over in Sidewinder. That suited him just fine. If he could not find the cannon and use Holtz's plan to blow open the safe in the bank, he would come up with some other scheme to get the money himself.

"It's the challenge," he told himself. That, and he had taken an instant dislike to the bank president. Butter wouldn't melt in Mort Thompson's mouth; then he would turn around and foreclose on a man's property if there was even one payment late.

"There you are, Jethro," called Dan Whitmore. The preacher waved him over. "I got a load of goods I need taken to the church. You're just the man to do it."

"I need to talk a moment," Slocum said, taking Preacher Dan aside. He explained his lack of funds and finished, "I'll do what I can to help with the building, but other than this, I don't want a whole lot to do with the sermons."

"If you work on the church, you should attend services," Preacher Dan said solemnly. "It's for the good of your immortal soul." When he saw Slocum was going to balk, he quickly added, "However, your effort in the name of the Lord will be appreciated greatly. A dollar a day and food. I suspect you can make your own arrangements where you sleep."

Slocum looked at Preacher Dan sharply, wondering if this was a broad hint that the man guessed Slocum was sleeping with his daughter. If Whitmore knew, he didn't give any sign of it bothering him much. Slocum had never seen a preacher and his daughter more ambivalent about the nature of sin. That suited him just fine.

"All of this?" Slocum looked at the pile of equipment, and wondered why Preacher Dan had bought so much wood already sawed to short lengths. The four-by-fours were hardly three feet long and not good for much of anything.

"All of it. There ought to be twenty of those," Preacher Dan said, pointing to the four-by-fours, "and all that planking."

"I hope you got it for a song and a dance," Slocum said, eyeing the planks. They had been cut into three-foot-wide pieces and none was longer than six feet. "That's going to take a whale of a lot of nailing to get put up. You should have bought bigger pieces."

"Donations," Preacher Dan said confidentially. "As the Good Book says, beggars can't be choosers."

Slocum wondered at this. For all the wood, there were few enough boxes of nails. Two kinds of shovels completed the order.

"I can carry it piecemeal or take most of it in one trip in the wagon."

"That won't be necessary," Preacher Dan said. "The owner offered the use of a barrow. Use that. No need to hurry. Just get it done before sundown. I'm holding a prayer meeting for all the volunteers—you need not come, Jethro, unless you want—and they can use the wood as crude pews."

Slocum didn't see it, but he was not going to argue. A dollar a day and food was coming his way for the easy work of moving sawed wood. He wheeled the barrow around, loaded the first of the short four-by-fours, and began wheeling them down to the church. As he returned for the second load, he saw Preacher Dan pressed up against a wall, a man stabbing his finger in Whitmore's chest.

"You are nothing but a charlatan, a poser, a pretender! You are the pawn of Satan!" The man shoved Whitmore back when he tried to escape and continued his tirade.

"Jethro. Jethro!" Preacher Dan waved to Slocum.

"What can I do for you?" Slocum asked. The man holding Preacher Dan against the wall did not budge. Slocum stepped up onto the boardwalk and moved in such a way that he crowded the man out. For a moment, Slocum thought he was going to have to fight. The man cocked his fist back as if he was ready to unload a haymaker, then stepped away.

"You bring out the worst in me," the man said.

"Let me guess," Slocum said. "Your name's Gantt, and you're the preacher in the church at the other end of town."

"Look at the kind of man you hire, Whitmore. He . . . he's nothing but a gunslinger!"

With that, Gantt swung about and stormed off, head high and shoulders squared.

"Righteous son of a bitch, isn't he?" Preacher Dan looked at Slocum the instant he spoke, and then smiled ingratiatingly. "Some folks bring out the worst in me," Preacher Dan mocked. "Turning the other cheek is hard sometimes."

Slocum shrugged and went back to work. Some minsters did a better job of living what they preached than others. He decided Preacher Dan was needing to do some work on this. As to Gantt, something had riled him. Slocum was not sure it was simply competition for his flock. Putting his back to it, Slocum pushed another load of four-by-fours down to the church where the carpenters worked diligently to erect the walls. He helped them raise one wall and nail it to support studs. Then he stood back and tried to figure what Preacher Dan was going to do with the short beams he had been hauling from the store. It hardly mattered that they were donations. They were useless, unless they were going to be stacked behind the church and used as firewood when the season changed.

Slocum returned to the store for the planks, and had just wrestled the last onto the barrow when the owner came bustling out.

"A minute, son," he said. "You the one who's supposed to pay me for those?"

"Pay? I thought the wood was all donated," Slocum said.

"If it is, it ain't my donatin'. I go to Reverend Gantt's church and ain't changin' my ways. If somebody else is footin' the bill for the wood, send 'em along to me so I can get paid. That's powerful expensive wood."

"You saw it up special?"

"Of course I did," the store owner said tartly. "Who in their right mind'd want four-by-fours cut to only three feet? No good for buildin' anythin' I ever heard of."

"Nope, reckon not," Slocum said. "I'll let Preacher Dan know you want your money when I see him."

"Do that. I'd like to see it in my cash drawer before I close."

Slocum saw that wouldn't be much longer. The sun was setting fast behind the mesa overlooking the town. He lifted the handles of the barrow and started it rolling to the church site. The carpenters had left for the day, so Slocum dumped the planks to one side of the church. He wiped sweat from his face, then remembered he had to return the barrow to the store.

As he wheeled it back, he saw Tessa juggling a stack of paper on the boardwalk across the street. She was so engrossed in finding one page and then moving it under others that she didn't notice him. Slocum picked up his pace, left the barrow leaning against the store wall, and went after her.

He was almost within distance to reach out and touch her shoulder when she did an abrupt right face and marched into a store. Slocum stopped in the doorway and took a deep whiff. Printer's ink. The clank of a printing press in the rear almost drowned out what Tessa was saying to the man wearing an apron and wiping his hands on a dirty rag.

The man took the pages from her and, holding them at arm's length, peered at them.

"You sure this is all true, miss?"

"Right as rain, Mr. Crawford. This is exactly the kind of reporting the *Bitter Springs Gazette* has been lacking."

"I'd need to be mighty sure before printing anything like this. It damn near accuses Gantt of being a crook."

"He *is* a crook, Mr. Crawford," she insisted. "See?" Her finger pointed to something on the page. Slocum wished he could see what it was. The newspaper editor's eyes grew wider, and then he laughed.

"I'll be switched. I knew he was too good to be true. The sanctimonious whoremonger!"

Slocum took a seat in a wicker chair beside the door so he could eavesdrop without being seen. Tessa had given the editor something about Gantt that sounded libelous. Slocum leaned back and pressed his ear against the wall to better hear over the clanking of the printing press.

"Rafe, stop printing the edition," Crawford called out. "We got to rewrite the headline."

"You mean the new church goin' up ain't our lead? That's 'bout all that's happened in Bitter Springs in the last six months worth the ink and paper."

"Rafe, do as I say. Get the type ready to set on a new story."

The printer's assistant grumbled, but Slocum heard the sounds of a printing press being dismantled to take off the printing plate.

"You want a job full-time?" Crawford walked across the print shop and sat at his desk. "You've got the makin's of a first-rate reporter."

"Oh, no, Mr. Crawford, this is just something I happened across. Why, I don't even want credit for it."

"No byline?" Crawford sounded hopeful at this. Slocum guessed that the editor didn't much like Gantt and wanted to take credit for the story.

"Why, no, I wouldn't know what to do with it," Tessa said ingenuously. "If you can use this, be my guest. Go ahead and do what you have to with it." She hesitated and then said, "Gracious me, I have to hurry. Do excuse me, Mr. Crawford."

"I got plenty of work to do resettin' the type," the editor muttered.

Tessa was already out the door when he called out his thanks. She walked past Slocum without seeing him, her pace rapid as she headed for the hotel. Slocum caught up quickly with her.

She jumped a foot when he touched her arm.

"Oh, John, you startled me. I wasn't expecting anyone to be so close by."

"I hope you won't jump at all my touches," he said.

"Oh, I don't know. I seem to remember getting really excited the last time you . . . touched me." Her eyes dipped down to his crotch to emphasize her words.

"Work's done for the day," he told her, watching her reaction.

"Oh, so is mine."

"Giving the editor of the town newspaper dirt on Gantt?"

She looked at him closely, then sidled up and put her hand on his chest. His heart beat a little quicker than before.

"We can talk about it later," she said. "Afterward."

"After what?"

"If you have to ask, you're not half the man I know you are." She slid her hand down his chest slowly and teased him with the briefest of touches at his groin. Slocum felt as if he were getting ready to turn cartwheels. He followed her into the hotel, then hesitated.

"Don't worry," she said softly. "The clerk is always drunk. See? He's already passed out." Tessa took Slocum by the hand and led him to the stairs going to the second floor. Every creak of the dried wood in the steps caused Slocum to wonder if the clerk would awaken and see them. It wouldn't do Tessa's reputation any good if it were known she was entertaining a man in her room at night. This was especially true since her pa was a preacher getting ready to build himself a church.

"Where's your pa?"

"Oh, out," she said vaguely. "Why ask about him?"

"I wouldn't want him to—"

"Then let's hurry," she said, turning the key in the lock and pulling Slocum into the room after her in one quick gesture. She kicked the door shut and locked it as she turned to him.

He pressed her against the door and felt her soft body yielding under his. For a moment, his green eyes stared into her blue ones. Then her eyelids drooped just a little in invitation. As her lips parted, he invited himself to the party.

Their lips crushed, and he felt her tongue begin to intrude into his mouth. He let it. Over and over, their oral organs dueled, moving in ways that he knew would be duplicated later—farther down on their bodies. He was so stiff in his jeans that he was getting uncomfortable.

Tessa sensed his problem. She pushed him away and sank down so she knelt in front of him. Her nimble fingers worked on his gun belt and then his fly.

"Oh, look what we have here. Is it cold?"

"It's burning up," Slocum said as she began stroking up and down his hardened shaft.

"Looks cold to me. Let me warm it up even more." She bent down and took him entirely into her mouth with one smooth movement. He felt the rubbery tip of his manhood bounce off the roof of her mouth and then go lower, deeper, into her throat. He almost lost control then and there. Reaching down, he stroked over her silky black hair, guiding her as she moved up and down on him. He had never felt a woman better able to take his length like this, and it sent shivers of desire throughout his loins.

"Umm, tasty," she said. "But how about putting it somewhere else to get really hot?"

"Where might that be?" he asked needlessly. Slocum was already lifting her up and turning her around. Tessa put her hands against the door and widened her stance as he lifted her skirts.

"I'm all ready for you," she said in a husky whisper. She leaned into the door now, spread-eagle and facing away from him. "I want you so, John. I want you now."

His fingers stroked up her legs, tracing over firm muscles and finally finding the curved, fleshy half-moons of her ass. He hiked her skirt up even more and placed both his hands on her buttocks. Kneading the twin mounds caused her to gasp and sob with need. In no hurry, he took his time to enjoy the silky flow of her skin under his fingers. Only when she went a little weak in the knees did he slip his hands around to her belly—and lower.

She cried out when he slid a finger into her wetness. He moved it slowly in and out until Tessa thrust herself back against him and begged for him to enter.

"Please, don't tease me. I want you inside me. I need you, John, I need you so!"

Pulling back on her hips molded her perfectly to his groin. His shaft parted the thick cheeks and then surged lower and forward to enter where his finger had been only moments before.

The sudden entry took both their breaths away. The heat and wetness and tightness all around him worked to make him lose his control. Slocum held on, and the urge subsided, but not the desire. He reveled in the feel of female flesh all around his length.

She began pushing hard against the door and thrusting herself back into him to make him sink even farther into her constricted passage. Slocum let her do this a few times, and then reached around her body to cup her breasts. Crushing down on them, pulling her toward him, he levered himself forward and sank balls-deep into her.

Tessa cried out and began quivering all over. He started a slow, methodical movement that quickly turned ragged as he was crushed flat by her strong inner muscles.

Pounding hard now, he slammed her repeatedly against the door. She shoved back as hard, grinding her hips around him until there was no turning back for either of them. She bent forward as far as she could and shoved her hips into him as he slipped powerfully forward. This triggered a carnal fire that consumed them both.

It was Slocum's turn to sag a little in the legs. He held on and swung Tessa about, and dropped her onto the bed in the small hotel room. He collapsed beside her. She lay stretched out on her back, legs dangling off the side of the bed and her arms high over her head.

He reached over and stroked across her still-hidden breasts.

"There are buttons," she said softly.

"You want me to unbutton your blouse?"

"I want you to rip it off!"

Like a tiger, she swarmed over him, ready for more. It was a while before he could deliver—but he did. All through the night he did, until the faint rays of sunlight poked through the window at dawn.

It was only when he felt a naked Tessa stirring in the circle of his arms that he remembered that she had never told him why she was working so hard to destroy Gantt's reputation. Then she awoke, and he forgot all about it again until he left her room, enjoying every instant of remembering how he had come to be so sore.

12

Slocum wandered around the construction site, wondering at how the church was proceeding. The walls had been pushed up into place and the roof needed to be nailed down. But this part did not make Slocum curious as much as the large pile of dirt behind the church. He remembered how the foundation had been dug down a ways, unlike most of the buildings in town. Some, like the saloon, could be dragged off if enough horses were yoked onto the building. Skids rather than solid foundations were the usual method of construction in Bitter Springs. Air flowed freely beneath, and let anything that might get dropped onto the floorboards seep through into the dirt.

But Whitmore had insisted on a foundation with the corners of the church driven down a ways into the ground to anchor it. Slocum scratched his head when he saw that the pile of four-by-fours was smaller than the day before. He had moved every last one of the wood beams and knew how many there had been. He walked through the shell of the church, hunting for the spot where the three-foot lengths had been used, and could not find it. More than that, some of the planks were missing, too. Slocum shrugged it off. People would steal anything, even from a church.

"Jethro!" called Preacher Dan. The man hurried over. "I was hunting for you." He looked a bit flustered.

"The construction getting you down?" Slocum asked.

"What? Why do you say that?" The man was thinner than before when Slocum had hitched a ride into town with him, and a tad on the pale side, as if he had the ague.

"This is a big project," Slocum said. He waved his hand about carelessly to see where Preacher Dan's eyes stopped. Slocum was disappointed that his ploy failed. The man's eyes never wavered from Slocum's.

"So it is."

"Looks like you've got a bit of thievery going on, too."

"How's that?"

Slocum saw how the preacher reacted, as if he had been caught at something immoral if not downright sinful.

"The wood beams, some planks. I can't see that they were used, and they're not on the pile outside." Slocum did not mention the extra dirt.

"Oh, those," Preacher Dan said in relief. "I traded a few items for nails. I had plumb forgot to get nails. How foolish of me, but you are right that this is a big project. I'm not used to such construction."

"Been giving your sermons out of the wagon for a spell?"

"Yes, that's right," Preacher Dan said. "I need you to go to the courthouse and find the deed to this property. There's a chance I don't have clear title to it as I had been promised. That's always the way when you're depending on donations."

"The land was donated? Like the wood?"

"I am very fortunate that the people of Bitter Springs are so generous," Preacher Dan said, his eyes going to the sky as he placed his hand over his heart.

"Why not ask the land office clerk to do the title search?"

"I'd like to keep this quiet in case the land's not free and clear. Then we can work to make things right. There's always a few folks in town willing to gum up the works."

"Gantt?"

"Among others," Whitmore said. His eyes darted across the street. The bank president stood just outside the door, watching closely everything that happened around the church.

"You and Thompson have a parting of the ways? He seemed to take to Tessa."

"Oh, no problem with the bank. Mr. Thompson has been quite generous offering a loan. I am trying to build the church without going into debt, and it looks as if we will make it. Unless the title is in question. Can you do that for me, Jethro?"

Slocum saw a few workers close by exchange looks. Whether they had overheard, Slocum couldn't say, but it was a good idea to have Preacher Dan continue calling him by the name Jethro. To change now in public would arouse suspicion, and suspicion would lead to someone making a query to the Texas Rangers. The last thing Slocum needed was a Ranger or two poking about and matching his description with the one Ranger Jeffers had undoubtedly given.

"I'll see what I can do," Slocum said, still wondering why Preacher Dan didn't send Tessa to do this errand. He smiled ruefully at the thought the woman might be too busy digging up dirt on Gantt and anyone else trying to block the new congregation. As Slocum walked away, he nodded in the banker's direction. He wasn't surprised when Thompson ignored him.

After all, Slocum was nothing more than a hired hand and beneath the notice of a rich, important citizen like a bank president. Slocum smiled. The gold in the safe—that should be in the safe, if Rebel Jack was right—would be removed one way or another. Slocum concocted plans that had nothing to do with using a cannon to blow open the safe. He needed to know under what circumstances Thompson opened the safe. That was the best time to strike. If he timed things right, he could rob the bank and be gone long before Holtz and his gang even knew the bank had been robbed.

Having the former Johnny Reb and his henchmen after

him was no worse than knowing the cavalry and the entire company of Texas Rangers wanted a piece of him. Slocum could dodge all of them just as easily as some. If he rode with saddlebags full of gold, that gave incentive.

Whistling tunelessly, he walked to the far side of town, turned away from Gantt's humble church, and went to a building only slightly more elegant where the town records were kept. Any trials were conducted in a saloon, and there wasn't a town marshal. All that kept Bitter Springs going was in this building—a mayor, a clerk or two, and whoever cleaned up the floors.

Slocum found the small room where the land office records were kept.

"Hello? Anybody around?" He went inside and peered down rows of records kept in bound volumes. Seeing the clerk was out, either on business or to grab a quick beer, Slocum began looking at the books holding the recorded land deeds. He had poked around in such files before, and quickly figured out the system used in Bitter Springs. Less than twenty minutes later, he had the information Preacher Dan wanted. Slocum scribbled down the pertinent record numbers and names and tucked the paper into his shirt pocket. His fingers lingered there a moment.

The money from the desert strongbox had been there. Now there was only that single scrap of paper. If he had kept riding, he wouldn't have gotten caught up in Rebel Jack's harebrained scheme and almost been killed in the mine. He shrugged off his bad luck. Toombs's cousin—if Josh was even that—had paid with his life for trying to kill him. Slocum called that even, but burning the money had been a blow.

"Money to burn," he said to himself. He had always wanted enough to use a bill to light a fancy cigar. There hadn't been a cigar, but the burning money had saved his life. Being content with that was all he could do.

He stopped in the doorway of the small records room and frowned. Something gnawed at the corners of his mind.

"Burned," he said, letting the word roll off his tongue.

He turned back into the records and began looking for something more this time. The record books for 1862 were sparse. He did find what he sought. The city tax records showed how much of the town had been destroyed as the Confederate troops withdrew. It took little for Slocum to read between the lines that the fighting had been fierce, and the small detachment of CSA soldiers had been routed at great expense to property in Bitter Springs.

A small scribbled notation at the bottom of one record brought a smile to Slocum's face. Jensen's pharmacy had been left untouched, not only because he was a Southern sympathizer but also because he supplied medicines to the Federals. The old man had successfully played both sides of the conflict. Slocum leafed through more volumes, and was interrupted when the clerk returned.

"What are you doin'?" the young man asked. He adjusted his celluloid collar and looked uneasy. Slocum guessed the man's lunch had been something more than a quick sandwich or bowl of stew. The way the man hitched up his pants suggested a tryst with some female companion had been on the menu.

"You were out with . . . her," Slocum said, "so I decided to start my search."

"Her?" the man said uneasily. "What do you mean?"

"You know who I mean," Slocum said, "and it doesn't bother me one jot. Can you tell me if Jensen's store has been moved since it was built?"

"She, I, uh, no," the young man stammered. "Jensen's pharmacy? It's been there since I got to town."

"How long's that been?" Slocum guessed the man was in his early twenties. The cannon would have been hidden back in '62.

"I was five. Just after Sibley's men blowed up the whole dang place. I still have nightmares."

"You're saying you got here seventeen years ago?"

"Maybe a tad more," the clerk said, still not happy with Slocum or his knowledge of what had been happening during the long lunch.

"Thanks," Slocum said. "I feel the need to get some headache powders."

"Don't expect much from Jensen. He's a crotchety old bastard."

"Yeah, but he's got medicine for the clap," Slocum said, winking to the clerk, who turned white with shock at the notion.

Slocum saw Tessa talking with the newspaper editor across the street, so he ducked down an alley and took a roundabout route to get to Jensen's store. He stared at the dilapidated building, then took a dozen steps back to get an even better look at it from the rear. Like most of the buildings in Bitter Springs, it had been built up off the ground to afford crawl space underneath. Slocum considered crawling around to see what was beneath the store, then shivered at the memory of being trapped in the mine.

He slowly walked around the building, and stopped when he came upon a large rock near the front door. Slocum went to it and saw a small brass plate had been mounted on the side with the date of Sibley's invasion. The words "NEVER FORGET" were scratched into the plate just above the date.

"Never forget," Slocum mused. He pressed his hand against the plate. After all the years, it was still fastened securely to the rock.

Looking around and not seeing anyone paying a bit of attention to him, Slocum took out his knife and drove the tip under one edge of the plate. He pried off the brass plate and then let out a sigh of resignation. Getting to this point had been easy, and he thought he would find a small cavity behind the plate with a map stuffed into it.

Bare rock met his gaze. He tapped the rock with his knife. Solid rock.

"I must be on the wrong track," Slocum said, putting the brass plate back. As he started to tap it into place with the butt end of his knife, he stopped and stared. Flipping the brass plate around and wiping off accumulated dirt made him whoop with glee.

Etched into the back of the plate was a crude map of

Bitter Springs. A prominent X drew his attention. Slocum oriented the metal map, and saw that the X indicated a spot on the western mesa overlooking town. If the Rebels had shelled the town, they would have created the most havoc firing from the heights.

"What you doin'? You lookin' to steal from me?" Jensen wobbled out of his pharmacy and peered nearsightedly at Slocum.

"Just taking a break," Slocum said. He moved so he could push the plate back into the rock where it had been. He had popped the screws used to hold it firmly into the rock, but doubted Jensen would notice.

"You're nothin' but a lazy layabout, takin' a break in the middle of the afternoon. I ought to tell that preacher fella about you. He'd fire your ass!"

"I'm sure he would," Slocum said.

"Git along and quit scarin' my customers off."

"If I scared any away, I'd be saving their lives," Slocum said.

"What's that? You insolent young pup! I tried to show you some charity. I let you drink with me, but you're like the rest of 'em. No loyalty!"

Slocum walked off, leaving Jensen to rant drunkenly about ingrates and customers who wouldn't pay. He slowed as he went by the church. The carpenters had left for the day, although there were still a couple hours of sunlight left. It might be the hottest part of the day, but Slocum could not believe they had taken a siesta and then would return at twilight to finish their work. He walked over as Preacher Dan came out from the husk of a church.

"Found the information," Slocum said. "Looks like you've got title free and clear."

"That's good to hear," the man said, distracted. He looked around and then behind him into the church.

"Is anything wrong?"

"What? Oh, no, nothing's wrong," Preacher Dan said. "Work is going well."

"So well that you sent the workmen home for the day?"

"They had done so much, and I need to get more supplies."

"Let me have the list, and I'll go get them now," Slocum offered.

"Oh, that's all right," Preacher Dan said hastily. "Tomorrow morning will be fine."

Slocum wondered what was wrong. If he fetched the building materials now, the workmen would have them when they showed up at dawn. If he took the time the next day to get the wood and whatever else Preacher Dan needed, the carpenters would sit around with nothing to do.

"Are you running out of money?"

"Of course not," the preacher said tartly. "There's more than enough in the bank to cover our expenses." Preacher Dan took a few steps, stopped, took a step to the side, and looked around.

"If you don't need me anymore, I have an errand to run," Slocum said. The preacher dismissed him with a wave of his hand. Whatever Dan Whitmore was doing looked like the dance of a prairie chicken. He stepped a few paces one way, then retreated and paced in another direction. Slocum thought the preacher might have a touch of sunstroke, but it wasn't his place to ask. If Tessa saw her pa acting strangely, she would be in a better position to do something about it.

Slocum considered finding her, then saw her coming down the street. He wanted to explore the mesa overlooking the town for sign of the cannon, so he took off at a brisk pace, acting as if he had not seen her. Having to deal with her pa's loco behavior and with the need to keep her occupied was solved by Slocum ducking around the back of the church.

Tessa came up and spoke several seconds with her father. Then the two of them started hopping about, moving hither and yon, pointing and exchanging hot words. Slocum couldn't hear from where he stood, and decided he did not want to know what went on. He went to the livery stables, got his mare, and was on his way out of town within a few minutes, heading along the road to Fort Suddereth.

The trail leading to the top of the mesa was soon apparent to him, and he turned up it. The mare balked at the sight of the steep route, but Slocum kept her moving and in no time they reached the tabletop of land.

Slocum pushed his hat back on his forehead and looked around. This was nothing like he expected. He had thought the Confederate artillerists would have wrestled their howitzer up the same trail he had taken. The back side of the mesa sloped down evenly toward the desert to the west. A heavily loaded caisson could follow the gun carriage up with little effort to a spot looking down on Bitter Springs. Slocum rode to the edge of the mesa and saw gas lamps lighted in windows of houses below.

He judged distances and range of war-era cannons, and decided this position would have been perfect for stopping Federal troops from rushing down from Fort Union, going down into Texas, and then circling around to attack Mesilla after General Sibley had left. If Mesilla surrendered quickly, the Union force could have followed Sibley north along the Rio Grande and cut off any possible retreat if he had faltered in his attack at Fort Craig or Albuquerque.

Satisfied that this was a tactical position even a green artillery officer would have selected, Slocum wheeled his horse around and studied the flat land. If the Confederates had abandoned their cannon and buried it here, as the etched brass map suggested, they would have chosen a spot easily found again. There would not have been time to do much elaborate camouflage. But even if the Federals were hot on their heels, they could have had time to dig a hole and cover up their howitzer.

Seventeen years of wind and rain would have erased obvious signs of where the soldiers had buried the artillery piece. But Slocum thought there had to be something still there that would mark the spot. He had started riding back and forth, looking for landmarks, when he heard the jingle of spurs and the loud neighing of a horse protesting the steep climb up from Bitter Springs.

He rode toward the head of the trail, then drew rein when the voices echoed up to him.

"You sure it's him, Heyward?"

"All I know is the description that cranky old bastard gave me," came a young voice that almost cracked. "Said the owlhoot was trying to steal a rock or something. I couldn't make head nor tail of his complaint, but the description's the one Jeffers posted."

Rangers.

Slocum wasted no time in turning his mare's head and starting down the back side of the mesa, its slope seeming more extreme now that he was on it. His horse slipped and skidded and kicked up a considerable cloud of dust. That it was almost dark made the descent more dangerous, but Slocum had no choice. When he got to the bottom of the incline, he put his heels to his horse and rocketed off.

"Stop, stop or we'll shoot!" came the faint command from behind. The Texas Rangers had spotted him right away and were in hot pursuit.

Slocum bent low and got his mare into a full-out gallop. He could not keep up this pace for more than a couple minutes, but he needed to put distance between himself and the lawmen so he could think.

Bullets tearing along after him kept him from doing too much more than ducking low and praying he could keep sufficient distance from the Rangers so they had no chance of hitting him. In the saddle, with their six-shooters blazing, only an accidental shot could get him. No man galloped and fired a handgun accurately.

The heavier, throatier report of a rifle caused him to bend even lower. A man astride a horse using a rifle was another kettle of fish. He had seen a Wild West show where a rider galloped full speed and shot clay pipes out of the mouths of his assistants. At the time, Slocum had wondered how many assistants the marksman had to hire in a year, but after that show there had been no need to wonder. He had shot eight clay pipes out of eight mouths with a single ride past.

Slocum considered getting off the road heading north and circling back to Bitter Springs. He discarded the idea quickly, though, when he knew how easy it would be to find him in the small town. Whose horse would be lathered? Only his. And Jensen had sent the Texas Rangers after him because he had been fiddling around with the brass plate. If the lawmen got too curious and examined the plate, they might figure out its importance.

Feeling his horse begin to tire under him, Slocum slowed the pace, and finally saw a small trail leading off the road. He trotted down it before realizing where it headed. If he kept on this trail, he would lead the Rangers directly into Rebel Jack's camp.

A wicked grin came to his lips. That might not be so bad. If the Rangers took out Jack Holtz, Slocum would have free rein to do as he pleased back in Bitter Springs. He might need some help, but there might be a way he could fire the cannon and still get the money from the bank safe.

"He's not far ahead, I tell you," came the adolescent voice of the Ranger named Heyward. Slocum wondered if the Ranger had owl eyes, able to see in the dark. He had thought the trail was well enough hidden that a casual rider would miss it out on the road. He had been wrong. Obviously. The Rangers pushed their horses harder than he could his mare.

Slocum looked up and saw how far he was from the outlaw camp. He could never get up the trail before the Rangers caught him. Whipping out his six-shooter, Slocum turned in the saddle and fired into the darkness behind him.

"Rangers!" he shouted. His warning echoed all the way down the narrow canyon, and had to reach the top of the mesa where Rebel Jack camped.

He fired until his six-gun came up empty, then sought a spot to make his stand. A rifle could either ventilate the Rangers or hold them at bay until Holtz sent his gang to investigate.

Slocum ruefully admitted he might be wrong. Hearing the warning, Holtz might simply climb on his horse and ride in the opposite direction. His gang would be at his heels.

Hitting the ground at a run, he stumbled and regained his balance in time to flop behind a large rock. He hefted his rifle and waited. A shadowy rider appeared on the trail. Slocum sighted and fired. And missed. The rider ducked low and wheeled his horse around.

"He's gone to ground, Heyward. Let's get him from both sides."

Slocum wondered at the older Ranger, who ought to be more experienced, shouting an order like that. Then he went cold inside. The Ranger was trying to flush him like a mourning dove. Slocum swung to his left and looked hard at the desert. Nothing moved. He spun around just as the crunch of boots on gravel alerted him. His rifle leveled on the young Ranger.

The man's eyes went wide.

"I didn't think you were here," the Ranger said. His voice broke.

"We're a-comin' to yer rescue!" The loud cry from higher on the mountainside told Slocum that Holtz's gang was willing to mix it up with Texas Rangers. Whether Rebel Jack had spurred them on with the promise that rescuing Slocum would get them the cannon needed to rob the bank, or whether they were only looking for a fight, he did not know. Four mounted men came down the trail from above.

"On your belly. Now!" Slocum snapped at the Ranger. The youngster dropped like a sack of suet.

The four outlaws rode past Slocum, intent on firing at the other Ranger, who had taken flight.

When Rebel Jack's henchmen were gone, chasing the other Ranger, Slocum went to the one he had caught.

He looked down at the Ranger in wonder. He was hardly eighteen, if that.

"You're mighty young to be a Ranger, aren't you?"

"Go on, get it over with."

Slocum stepped up and kicked hard, sending the six-shooter in the boy's hand flying.

"You can kill me now. I'm unarmed."

"Maybe I would have killed you if you hadn't tried to shoot me," Slocum said. "I like a man with spunk. Get up."

"I'd rather die facing the man who cut me down."

"You've got too many romantic notions in that thick head of yours. Get rid of them," Slocum said. "Get rid of them and maybe you'll live a long life."

"You're not going to kill me?" The Ranger sounded incredulous.

"I don't shoot unarmed men," Slocum said. "Take off before the others return. They wouldn't hesitate to put a few slugs into you."

"Why are you letting me go?"

"Why are you trying to talk me out of it?" Slocum shot back. He lifted his rifle and pointed out into the desert in the general direction of Bitter Springs. "If you hurry, you can get back to town before dawn."

The young man turned and started off, obviously expecting to get shot in the back. When he realized this wasn't going to happen, he walked faster, head held high.

Slocum lifted his rifle and fired.

13

"Did you get him, Slocum?"

Slocum looked over his shoulder at Rebel Jack Holtz, sitting astride his horse. Lowering his rifle, he turned and nodded.

"Let's go see how good your shot was."

"I got him," Slocum said.

"Nevertheless, I want to see," Holtz insisted. "You were a top-notch sniper. It always pleases me to see an expert at work."

"I got him," Slocum repeated. He moved as Holtz started to ride past to go find the Ranger's body. "Are you saying I didn't?"

"What's got you so hot under the collar?"

"Hey, Jack," called an outlaw from the distant road. "The son of a bitch got away."

"What? How'd that happen?" Rebel Jack sawed at his reins and trotted a skittish horse to the road. Slocum lifted his rifle and considered what a single shot might do for his future. He lowered the Winchester and found his mare. He swung into the saddle about the time Rebel Jack returned, looking like a storm had settled over his head.

"Those idiots," the outlaw leader raged. "They let him get away. We got a Ranger runnin' around loose."

"There's an entire company of Rangers down in Sidewinder," Slocum pointed out. "This is going to make it really hot around here."

"They got other troubles," Holtz said after thinking on it. "All they know is that one of their boys got gunned down. You did a good job, Slocum, but it might mean a whale of a lot of trouble for us."

"The company's in Sidewinder to fight Indians," Slocum said. "Any word on the Warm Springs Apaches who left their reservation over in Arizona?"

"We don't hear much gossip out in the tules," Holtz said. "I don't like the men goin' into Bitter Springs, not after you cut down Rufus Toombs."

"Smart," Slocum said. "If the Rangers spot any of the gang there, all hell would break loose, and I'd never be able to show you where the cannon is hidden." Slocum waited for Holtz to understand what had just been said. It took only an instant.

"You found it? You got the cannon? Whoopee!"

"Hold your horses," Slocum cautioned. "I found the map, but the Rangers came after me before I could dig up the cannon."

"But you know where it is? Tell me about it!"

"Let's get on back to camp, and I'll lay out what I know," Slocum said. He looked over his shoulder in the direction taken by the young Ranger, Heyward. Nothing moved out there. Good.

"You yahoos keep huntin' for the Ranger," Holtz shouted.

"What good's that going to do?" Slocum asked. "He's long gone. If they rile up the dust on the road, it'll make finding our camp all the easier."

Holtz grumbled, then countered his own order and got the line of four outlaws moving up the trail ahead of him and Slocum. As they rode, Slocum listened to Holtz complaining about damn near everything, including how so many of his gang had lit out like scalded dogs. The four on the trail were the only ones remaining loyal to Holtz.

"Makes for more money when we divvy it up," Slocum said.

"Right," Holtz said. The tone Holtz used told Slocum a double cross was in the works. If he helped Holtz and his men get the gold from the bank, he was likely to find himself holding an empty bag—and maybe end up the scapegoat for the entire robbery. Holtz was not likely to shed many tears if Slocum was nabbed by the Texas Rangers while the Rebel got away with the stolen gold.

They settled into the camp, Holtz sending the other four out to stand watch. All protested, making Slocum think they would be less than observant once they reached their posts. The chance that the Rangers would come riding into camp was slim, though, and Slocum listened to both the complaints and Rebel Jack's arguments for vigilance with half an ear.

He poked at the campfire and watched the embers dance about. As hot as it was during the day in the desert, it got mighty cold at night. He warmed his hands, and then added a few twigs to build the heat.

"Where is it, Slocum? The sooner we get it set up, the quicker we'll be rich men." Holtz rubbed his hands together more from the thoughts of riches than any need to warm them.

"I found the map on the back of a brass plaque," Slocum explained. "The cannon has to be buried on the mesa overlooking the town."

"That'd give us a clear shot at the bank. Can you do it?"

"We'll need cannonballs and shot. And wadding. And unless they buried the fuses and rams alongside, we'll need all that, too," Slocum said.

"We can come by that. All except maybe the cannonballs."

"It wasn't hard to get the cannon to the top of the mesa. It wouldn't have been much harder to get a caisson up there, too. I suspect they buried everything we'll need, except the gunpowder. If they buried a couple kegs alongside the cannon, it might be worthless by now." Slocum knew the sun beating down, even on buried black powder, would do more to ruin it than storing it in a cool, dark place like the bottom of a mine shaft. He had been lucky once. He doubted it would happen again that he found all the powder he wanted exactly where he needed it most.

"I've got that taken care of," Holtz said.

"Then all we need to do is figure out where on that mesa Sibley's raiders buried their artillery."

"Do you think there might be another map? Something showing the exact location instead of just a general one?"

Slocum looked at Holtz, wondering if the man actually believed him. In the brief time during the war that their paths had crossed, Holtz had always been suspicious of everyone around him. It might have kept him alive then, but made for an undesirable trait in a partner now.

"Could be," Slocum said slowly. "You know something I don't?"

"Just heard rumors, nothing more," Holtz assured him.

"If I was an officer in charge of a battery, I'd hide my cannon where anyone could find it—if he was hunting for it."

"So you think the cannon is on the mesa in some place where it would be obvious to dig?"

"Something like that," Slocum said. "I didn't get a good look around, but there must be some markers that wouldn't weather away. A pile of rocks, a place where shadows cross, something."

"Shadows," muttered Holtz. "If I was hightailin' it and had to leave behind my guns, I'd use something at sundown to mark it. The shadows of distant mountains maybe."

"What time of year was it? The sun moves all around from summer to winter."

"Dang," cried Holtz. "I don't rightly know. If it wasn't right now, finding it will be impossible unless we wait for the right time of year."

"I want to look around some more before we go cutting

our own throats out of despair," Slocum said. "You got any food? My belly's rubbing up against my backbone it's been so long since I ate."

"Look around real good, men," Holtz ordered his henchmen. "Slocum says the cannon is buried somewhere on this mesa."

"What if it ain't? Then we'd be wastin' our time," griped one gunman. He rested his hand on the butt of his six-shooter in a way that made Slocum wonder if he intended to draw and fire. Whether his target would be Holtz or him, Slocum did not want to predict. If there was so much as a twitch in the man's gun hand, Slocum intended to draw and shoot to kill.

The four in Holtz's gang had done nothing but complain from the time they broke camp. Holtz had tried to explain to them the Rangers would come swooping down on their camp as soon as they got a few men together from the Sidewinder company. The outlaws had not sounded convinced as they rode out, grumbling all the way.

"What do you want them to do, Slocum?" Rebel Jack eyed Slocum closely.

Slocum turned in a full circle, taking in the expanse of the mesa above Bitter Springs. He saw nothing that suggested a good spot to dig, much less markers the soldiers would have used to show where they hid the cannon.

"Have them spread out and look around. There might be some kind of spike driven into the ground."

"That wouldn't be around so long after they left. The dust would have covered it up," Holtz said.

"Might be we have to ask the pharmacist down in the town a few questions. He was around when the fighting went on, and he put the plaque with the map onto the rock."

"Sounds like we can beat an answer or two out of him," Holtz said, warming to the notion of some violence against civilians. He had not changed much since the war.

"Hey, Jack, come take a look," called one of his men. He pointed at the ground. "This look like anything important?"

Holtz ran over. Slocum followed more slowly, getting his bearings. Where Holtz was digging around in the dirt was not a spot Slocum would have chosen to bury a cannon. There was nothing significant about it. He had the feeling the gun crew had found a spot that ought to be obvious to any other Rebel gunner who returned hunting for the cannon.

"Lookee here," Holtz said, holding up a silver dollar. "Some cowhand dropped a cartwheel." He scowled as he flipped it to the man who had found it. "That look like a damned cannon?"

"It was shiny, Jack. I thought—"

"You thought? You never had a thought in all your born days," raged Holtz.

"Keep looking," Slocum said. He didn't much care if Holtz and his henchman shot it out. He did care about finding the cannon. The more he walked around, the more he felt this was the right place. There was no question that the mesa commanded the town, and the roads coming from both south and north afforded easy access. This was a perfect spot.

Slocum turned and looked back down the slope to the west leading from the mesa top. He might have been wrong about what the map meant. It could have been nothing more than instructions copied from orders on where to put a gun emplacement. The artillerists might have retreated with their cannon and hidden—or abandoned—the field piece somewhere west of here. They might have, but it didn't seem right to Slocum.

He suspected the gun was here, if it was anywhere. Jensen would not have bothered with the map on the brass plate otherwise.

Carefully pacing from one side to the other did not reveal anything that struck him as important. Holtz and his four men were less diligent about their hunt. The four often clustered together, whispering among themselves. Slocum watched them closely, ready to shoot it out if they took it into their heads to reduce the number of shares again by killing him. After a half hour of searching, Slocum thought Rebel Jack might be a more likely target. The four gunmen watched him far more closely than they did Slocum.

After another half hour, the sun had risen high enough in the sky to make existence unbearable. The four went to Holtz and spoke for some time. Slocum guessed what they were talking over and it did not please him.

"Slocum," Rebel Jack said, coming up and putting an arm around his shoulders. Slocum shrugged off the arm and stepped away. "The boys got a problem hunting without actually seeing the map. It'd go a ways toward keepin' them happy if we could all take a gander at it."

"Down there," Slocum said pointing over the edge of the mesa. "Behind the brass plaque on the rock."

"We're not doubting you none. Might be you got it wrong."

"The only way I might have got it wrong is . . ." Slocum's voice trailed off.

"Yeah? What just occurred to you?"

"Might be the X marked a different spot than up here on the mesa," Slocum said. "Might be a way of indicating a point on the front of the plaque."

"Let's mosey on down and see." Holtz motioned for his men to mount up. They rode down to Bitter Springs in silence. Slocum thought hard all the way down. He did not think he was wrong that the howitzer was hidden on the mesa, but the idea that the X marked something on the front of the plaque seemed more and more likely after their futile hunt. They dismounted in front of Jensen's pharmacy. Slocum was happy to see that the old codger stayed inside. Or maybe, at this time of the afternoon, he made the rounds of the saloons and was getting himself knee-walking drunk.

"There it is," Slocum said, pointing to the large rock.

"Who'da thought to put a map in plain sight?" Holtz reached behind him and pulled out his knife from a sheath stuck in his belt. The plate popped off easily. He held it up as he stared at the back in the bright sunlight. "Damn me if you weren't right, Slocum. This is a map and it shows the cannon must be up on the mesa."

"We didn't find nuthin' there, Jack. We ain't diggin' up there without knowin' *exactly* where we're diggin'."

"Let me see it," Slocum said, taking the brass plate from Holtz. Slocum turned it over and looked at the inscription on the front, then matched the X on the back with letters.

"What do you think?" asked Holtz.

"The tops of the X would touch the first letters of 'NEVER' and 'FORGET' if it had been drawn on the front instead of the back." The bottoms of the X marked nothing but blank plate.

"NF? What does that mean?"

"It can mean anything, anything at all," said another of Holtz's gang.

"Could be someone's initials," Holtz said, ignoring the protests.

"There's no way to tell without asking somebody who's been here a long time." He thought of Jensen, then realized asking anything of the alcoholic pharmacist would be like poking a hornet's nest with a stick. There'd be a lot of buzzing, then they'd all get stung. A slow smile came to his lips. "There's somebody else I know who's been here long enough to know."

Slocum set off for the courthouse, and never slowed as he went into the file room. The clerk looked up, annoyed. Then he looked scared when he saw Holtz and his men crowding behind Slocum.

"Wh-what do you want? I thought you was headin' out of town."

"Came back. I need more information," Slocum said. The man motioned toward the record books. Slocum shook his head. "Not the kind of information I need. You were here when Sibley's troops retreated."

"Y-yes." The man turned paler when Rebel Jack Holtz came around, swung up his sawed-off shotgun, and laid it on the counter so the muzzle pointed in the clerk's general direction.

"What do you remember from back then of anything with the initials NF?"

"NF? That somebody's name? Or a business? A ranch?"

"Any of those. You tell me," Slocum said. He put his hand over Holtz's shotgun to keep the hotheaded rebel from lifting it and firing into the clerk.

"Y-your friend's a bit edgy, ain't he?"

"You might say that. NF. Who lived in Bitter Springs then with those initials?"

"I can't remember. I was only a small kid. How can I remember something that long back?" The clerk paled when Slocum took his hand off Holtz's shotgun. "Wait," the clerk blurted. "There might be—yeah, I know! NF. The New Frontier!"

"What's that?"

"The saloon at the end of town."

"Still run by the same gents?" Slocum asked.

"Don't think so, but the current owner's been serving his swill for more than ten years. Can't rightly say more."

"Gentlemen," Slocum said, "let's have a drink at the New Frontier." Slocum looked at the clerk, who shook visibly at the sight of Holtz and his gang. "You want to join us?"

Slocum laughed when the clerk shook his head.

Slocum led the way from the clerk's office. It was about time to wet his whistle—and find the cannon.

14

"Don't cause any trouble," Rebel Jack Holtz warned his men as they crowded into the New Frontier Drinking Emporium. They shoved and pushed and made a rush to the bar. The barkeep gave them the once-over, then served the beers they ordered, watching closely to be sure they all put their nickels on the bar before he was satisfied.

Slocum and Holtz took a table at the rear of the saloon. The bartender ignored them. This was fine with Slocum, but Holtz started to protest. Slocum grabbed his arm and pulled him back.

"We can drink later," Slocum said. "While we've still got clear heads, let's figure out where the cannon might be."

"Here!" Holtz waved his arms like a windmill, but settled down. He thought a moment, then added, "The barkeep knows. That chickenshit clerk said he was the owner, so he'd know."

"I doubt he keeps a Rebel cannon under his bar," Slocum said. "Chances are good he doesn't even know he has it."

"How can that be, Slocum? You're not pullin' anything funny, are you?" Holtz glared at him. Slocum saw the hair-trigger temper and the possibility of instant death in the outlaw's eyes.

"I want what's in the safe," Slocum said softly. "Working with you is the only way to get it." As much as the words burned Slocum's tongue as he spoke, it was the truth. Even if he found the cannon on his own, firing it accurately took several men in a crew working together. If they didn't find the cannon, Slocum was willing to think on other ways to blow open the safe. Having Holtz and his men help was a quicker way to ill-gotten wealth.

"What do you mean he maybe doesn't know he has it?"

"It might be buried under the saloon," Slocum said. "The man's only owned the place ten years. Seventeen years ago was when the Rebs buried the cannon."

"So if he doesn't know, what are we going to do?"

"Well," Slocum said, staring at the barkeep and the way he kept an eagle eye on the four outlaws at the bar, "your men look capable of keeping him occupied. Let's you and me do some poking around."

Slocum did not wait to see if Holtz was with him. He slipped out the back door and looked hard at the saloon and the way it had been built. Like most other buildings he had seen in Bitter Springs, this one was built on skids, providing a small crawl space underneath.

"Under the damned saloon?" Holtz grumbled.

"Maybe not," Slocum said, looking behind the building. "See how the entire saloon slid down from higher on the slope? At one time, the saloon had been fetched up against the tall cliff on the east side of town. Rain, too many men in the saloon, who knows? It slid downhill."

"Might be the road got moved, too," Holtz said, walking around. "See here? There's still a trace of an old road going here." He pointed to the ancient tracks.

Slocum walked to the edge of the cliff, and then turned in the direction of the saloon and saw evidence of the skid marks. He dropped to all fours and began looking more carefully at the ground. When he found a spot where the saloon had once rested, he looked up.

"You find something, Slocum?" Holtz ran over. "I didn't find squat."

"What do you make of this?" Slocum pointed to a discolored section of the ground. "It's not rock. It's dirt, but it's been packed down hard over the years."

"We found it," Holtz chortled. "We damned well found it!"

"We found something," Slocum said. He looked back toward Bitter Springs and the mesa rising up in the distance. That was the spot where he felt in his gut that the cannon had been buried, but this was a more promising place to dig.

"I'll get the fools out of the saloon and—"

"Let them finish their beers," Slocum said. "We should dig here when it gets dark so nobody will see us and ask questions."

"But—"

"But you can buy me a drink to celebrate," Slocum said. "By the time we're done, it'll be dark and we can get started." Slocum saw how eager Holtz was to get on with the excavation, but he held back his desire to do it and maybe have to shoot someone trying to stop them. As they went back into the saloon, other worries came to Slocum. When they unearthed the cannon, how would they move it? The undercarriage would have rotted away after so many years, even in the dry Texas desert.

He shrugged it off. That was a problem to solve when they got to it. A more immediate one was getting Holtz to pay for a shot of whiskey.

"Yes, sir, this is the place. I feel it in my bones," Holtz said as he leaned on a shovel. His men worked sporadically, digging in the sunbaked ground all around while Slocum dug with a steadiness that accomplished more than any two of the others.

"It looks different here. Even in the moonlight, I can see it," Slocum said, continuing to dig. Holtz was right. In the silver light cast by the almost-full moon, a distinct rectangle appeared to jump up out of the desert, showing something had been buried here.

"You figure out how to move the cannon when we get it all dug up?" Holtz asked.

Slocum stepped up out of the two-foot-deep pit they had already excavated and took a deep breath. Something was wrong, and he could not put his finger on it.

"I can borrow a wagon," he said, thinking of Preacher Dan's enclosed wagon. "We load the cannon barrel in, take it up to the mesa, and there we rig a carriage for it. No need to put it on fancy wheels since we're not taking it with us after we fire it."

"Can we fire it after so long?" asked Holtz. He turned to his men and barked, "Keep diggin', damn your eyes. We don't have all night. If anybody sees us, we're done for."

The men grumbled as was their wont, but put their backs into the digging.

"It might take a bit of renovation," Slocum admitted.

"Renovation? You make it sound like some kind of house. This is metal, Slocum, iron! It rusts."

"We'll know when we find it," was all Slocum could say. His nose wrinkled, and he turned away from the pit. He coughed and then almost gagged. Something was very wrong.

"My God, Jack, we're sinkin'!" The four men leaped from the pit and thrashed about. "It's all over our boots. And the goddamn stink!"

Slocum pulled up his bandanna to keep the smell from making him puke.

"They didn't bury no cannon here," one of Holtz's men said. "This is an outhouse that got covered up. We're diggin' down into shit!"

Slocum had to keep from laughing. What the outlaw said was true. He should have realized a saloon would have an outhouse behind it. When the road was moved and the saloon pulled along to remain near it, they had left the outhouse behind. At some point, it had been filled in and a new one dug closer to the saloon.

"You mean we aren't gonna find the cannon here?"

asked another of the outlaws. "We been wastin' our time! And for what!"

"You got a couple beers under your belts," Slocum said.

"That's it, Jack. We quit. We're not havin' no part in this no more!"

"Wait, you can't. This was a mistake."

While Rebel Jack went to sweet-talk his furious men, Slocum stepped away from the honey pit and found himself staring at the mesa to the west of town again. The brass plaque had indicated the cannon was up there. At least, he had interpreted the memorial map that way. Why else hide the map on the back of the brass plate if it didn't lead to something important?

Slocum had thought the cannon was up on the mesa. Now he was sure of it. Every instinct told him so.

"We're gettin' on our horses and leavin'."

"Wait, we can talk this out." Holtz stopped. His hand went to his six-gun, but Slocum clamped his hand around the outlaw's brawny wrist and kept him from shooting his own men.

"Let them go," Slocum said. "Gunplay would only draw unwanted attention."

"Yeah," Rebel Jack said coldly. "How would we explain digging up an abandoned outhouse?"

He jerked free of Slocum's grip and joined his men. The five rode back to the road and headed north. Slocum gathered the abandoned shovels and lashed them together. He intended to do some digging of his own up on the mesa.

Barely had he swung into the saddle when Holtz rode back at a gallop. The outlaw smiled ear to ear.

"They're sticking with us," Holtz said.

"Your men? What'd you say to them?"

"Not a damn thing. We was ridin' on out of town when a heavy wagon rumbled up. That bank president came out and ushered a squad of soldiers inside. They commenced to unloading more gold than I've ever seen in my life. The boys saw it, too. The army done us a big favor, Slocum. They gave an incentive for the men to stay with us."

"We still don't have a cannon," Slocum said.

"I'll get the men settled in a new camp and smooth their ruffled feathers. By morning, they'll be rarin' to dig up the whole damn town, if it gets them a piece of that gold. I do declare, there must have been ten thousand dollars worth in that shipment. We're going to be rich men, Slocum, rich!"

With that, Holtz turned his horse and galloped back to join his men, leaving Slocum alone with the shovels. Slocum followed more slowly, not wanting to add to the clamor in the streets that might draw unwanted attention. The stench from the outhouse pit they had opened might go a ways toward stirring up the local citizens. There was no need to let anyone know who was responsible.

Slocum rode up behind Preacher Dan's half-built church and watched the soldiers finish unloading the gold. They piled into the wagon after Mort Thompson had left the bank, locking the front door. Slocum knew this was only a symbol of the bank's safety. The incredible, thick-walled iron safe inside provided the real security. Thompson walked away, whistling tunelessly.

The soldiers rattled on in their wagon, heading back north to Fort Union. Slocum itched to break into the bank then and there and try his hand at opening the safe by himself. Some dynamite would work miracles, though it would take considerable time to set the charge and then blow the safe. By that time, Thompson could have recruited a vigilance committee or sent for the company of Texas Rangers down in Sidewinder. More likely, a troop of cavalry would be dispatched from Fort Suddereth to look after their gold.

Slocum needed help getting into that safe. Holtz and his gang were a part of it, but the cannon gave Slocum the greatest hope of success. He looked behind him at the mesa and decided to go up and poke around while the moonlight illuminated the mesa as if it were day.

As he started to leave, he reined back and listened hard. He heard something far away, almost beyond the limits of his keen hearing. He looked around, trying to figure out what he was listening to. He failed. The noise was a scraping sound, a crunching, and then something like wood creaking. Slocum rode back to the church and looked into the shell. No work had been done today on the church. It still lacked a roof, but the walls were up and securely nailed into place.

Seeing no one poking about to make such noise, and thinking the sound must be coming from somewhere else in Bitter Springs, Slocum rode away. He was familiar with every murmur out in the desert or up in the mountains. Around towns, the noises became strange and unidentifiable to him. He preferred the sounds of coyotes and snakes slithering along and the wind blowing through vegetation to the odd creaks and moans of poorly built houses settling.

Slocum noticed how the shovels he had strapped to the back of his saddle clanked and scraped as he rode, adding to the odd sounds in the town. Soon enough, he was out of town and on the path leading up to the mesa. Within half an hour, he stood once more where he and Holtz's gang had hunted futilely for the hidden cannon. More than the feeling in his gut told him he was in the right place. Interpreting the brass plaque as projecting onto the front and inventing a place for the burial down in Bitter Springs had been wrong.

The gang members had demanded it, though, and Slocum knew Holtz had gone along. That showed how little real control Holtz had over his men. Most of the gang had left. If Holtz's fiery temper flared, he might find himself getting shot in the back or waking up one morning and finding all his gang gone.

He was no more able a leader now than he had been during the war.

In the silence of the mesa, bathed in liquid silver light, Slocum walked around aimlessly, looking this way and that for some notion as to how the Southern artillerists must have reacted seventeen years earlier.

At the edge of the mesa, he looked down into Bitter Springs. The town itself had migrated and grown a little, but not too much. If the battery officer had wanted to command

the heights, the cannon would have been set up about where
Slocum stood. He turned away from the town and looked
across the mesa. In the paler moonlight he saw something he
had missed in the bright sunlight. Small boulders produced a
definite shadow across the land. He shifted position and the
shadows moved. Not knowing when Sibley's detachment
had been here made depending on shadows a chancy proposition, but a slow smile came to Slocum's lips when he realized he was looking at the result, not the cause.

Shadows depended on the location of the sun or moon.
What cast the shadows were stationary. He walked along
one small ridge, retraced his steps, and took a few paces
along another. Then he came back to the spot where the
two minuscule ridges intersected.

"X marks the spot," he said. Using a shovel from the
stack he had brought, Slocum began digging. It was hard
work, and the dirt had settled and baked in the sun over almost two decades. About the time he was ready to give up
and simply ride down the western slope of the mesa for El
Paso, the tip of the shovel hit something hard.

Slocum had not found many rocks as he dug, and those
had been smaller than his fist. This was more substantial.
He worked his way along the obstruction, and within another twenty minutes a whoop of glee escaped his lips.

He had found the cannon buried about three feet below
the surface. Slocum wiped the sweat off his forehead, then
got to work. In an hour, he unearthed the cannon and had
dug around it enough so he could reach under the barrel.
His shovel hit something that made a dull thud as he tried
to lever the gun upward. Digging more furiously, he got
around and under the barrel and found a second cannon.
Jensen had not been blowing smoke out his ass about a second cannon. Both were buried in the same hole.

Slocum threw down his shovel and sat on the edge of
the excavation pit. He stared down at the two guns. He remembered seeing other guns like them at more than one
battle during the war. Once, he had even commanded a
battery and knew the guns intimately as a result. Best of

all, the bronze barrels were intact. The artillerists had rammed wadding into the mouth of both cannons to keep the dirt out. Bronze did not rust.

All he needed were strong backs to pull the two cannons from their grave and some gunpowder and shot to resurrect them.

A test firing or two to get the range, and the Bitter Springs bank would be blown apart—and with it the safe. He was on the verge of being very rich.

15

Slocum walked back to the edge of the mesa and stared down at the peaceful little town. His eyes fixed on one building, though. Preacher Dan's fledgling church. It needed a steeple and a roof; otherwise, the walls were ready for services. And it was in a direct line with the bank. One cannonball flying too short in its trajectory to the bank would blow up the church and anyone inside.

Slocum had not considered the church being an obstacle until this moment. Was a wagon creaking under a load of gold worth destroying the preacher's dream? If only Whitmore had built somewhere else rather than across the street from the bank, there would not be any problem.

But there was. Slocum had to think this through. If he told Holtz of his discovery, the outlaw would want to rob the bank immediately. That, Slocum knew, was the smart thing to do. They had no idea how long the army's gold would remain in the bank safe. Expenses for supplies and payroll at Fort Suddereth might deplete the account in a few days. Waiting for a second shipment of gold to match this one might require a month of lying low. Slocum doubted Holtz and his gang were capable of biding their time. They were an impatient bunch, always arguing among themselves and getting into trouble in spite of the golden carrot at the end of the stick. The way they had let the Texas Ranger escape had endangered the location of the camp.

Slocum wanted the gold in the bank, but he did not want to blow up Dan and Tessa Whitmore along with the safe. Brushing off his clothes, he mounted and retraced the trail back down into Bitter Springs. By the time he reached the half-built church, the sun was poking up over the mountains.

"Preacher Dan!" Slocum called, seeing the man poking about inside the church. "I need to talk to you."

"I'm busy, Jethro," Preacher Dan said.

"You look like you're fixing to die," Slocum said. The man was disheveled, dirty, and ten pounds thinner than when he had arrived in Bitter Springs. "Are you sick?"

"Only in the spirit. I strive to put patches on my immortal soul, but sometimes I fear it is a losing battle and that I am sinking into a sea of sin."

Slocum stared at him and shook his head. Preacher Dan walked with a limp now, and might have been with Holtz's gang as they dug up the outhouse for all the dirt and grime caked on him. All that was missing was the stench.

"Come along, son," Preacher Dan said, pushing Slocum away from the church. "It's breakfast time. I need to eat. You have been skipping meals, too, from the look of it."

Slocum realized he was hardly in any better condition than the preacher.

"I need to talk to you," Slocum said.

"Over breakfast. I'm famished. I . . . I've been working in the church and need some food." Whitmore wiped his hands on already filthy clothes. Slocum saw popped blisters on the man's hands and wondered what he might have been doing. All the heavy work had been done on the walls. Lifting the roof into place would take both skill and the hard work of a dozen or more men. It was not something a single man, even one of faith, could do.

"I'm a bit short on money," Slocum said.

"I'll buy, Jethro," Preacher Dan said loudly as they

passed by two men hurrying along on their way to work. Both had the look of clerks, and Slocum saw them go into the mercantile. Business must be good for the owner to need a pair of clerks.

"There's a shipment coming in today from up north," Preacher Dan said, seeing Slocum's interest. "They have to unload a considerable amount of freight destined for Fort Suddereth."

"Do tell," Slocum said, his own thoughts turning to the gold in the bank's safe. Purchases by the sutler and quartermaster down at Fort Suddereth meant the gold would be gone and put into the pocket of the mercantile's owner. At that thought, he smiled. What would the owner of the general store do with the gold? He would leave it where it was until he had to pay his own bills. The gold wasn't going to leave the bank, not for a few days.

"Order what you want," Preacher Dan said, motioning to the waiter.

"Morning, Dan," the waiter greeted. "The usual?"

"A steak sounds like the very thing I need," Preacher Dan said.

"Same," Slocum said. The waiter hesitated. "He's paying for it," Slocum added when he realized how disreputable he looked.

"That's the problem," said the waiter. "You really ought to pay some of what you owe on your bill, Dan. It's gettin' mighty high since you ain't paid since that first day you come to town."

"When the church is finished, I'll be in a better position to pay. When parishioners flock in—"

"I kin feed you today, but no more. Not till you pay something."

Slocum watched Preacher Dan closely. The man ought to have been a poker player for all the expression on his face.

"I will see what can be done. Thank you, my son."

The waiter left, muttering to himself. When he was out of earshot, Slocum said his piece.

"I think you ought to be out of town for a spell," Slocum said.

"Why is that?"

Slocum could not tell the preacher what was going to happen. If he did and Preacher Dan said nothing, he would be an accomplice. More likely, he would try to talk Slocum out of the robbery. Neither was productive. Slocum fell silent, wondering why he bothered. Then he remembered what the trajectory of a cannonball would look like from the mesa. He was not the best artilleryman in the country. He had been more than happy to return to being a sniper and then a scout after an uninspired turn as an artillery officer. A few shots to determine range would be necessary before hitting the safe squarely. At least one of those shots was likely to fall short—and land smack in the middle of Preacher Dan's church.

"I appreciate what you've done for me. You kept me from spending a long time in the Fort Suddereth stockade," he said. "Don't ask why. Just take a few days off from working on the church. You and Tessa go down to Fort Suddereth maybe."

"Or Sidewinder? Where the company of Texas Rangers makes their headquarters?"

Slocum knew he was being poked to see what his reaction would be.

"That'd be fine, too," he said in a level voice. He pushed back from the table when the waiter came with the steaks. Barely had the waiter left than Slocum drew closer and picked up knife and fork. His mouth watered at the sight and smell of so much beef. He missed being on a trail crew herding cattle. There was always enough steak for hungry cowboys. All they had to do was pick one from the herd and butcher it for enough meat to last days. Since leaving the Double Cross, he had seen little enough meat that didn't have mold on it.

"They surely do serve up good food here," Preacher Dan said, diving into his steak. Between bites, he asked, "Why do you want us out of town, Mr. Slocum?"

Using his real name brought Slocum up short. He could not tell the man.

"For a couple days. That's all I'm asking. Things are . . . happening." He knew how lame this sounded and how unconvincing it must be.

"After I get the church finished. Or is that going to be too late to avoid whatever problems you see coming to Bitter Springs?"

"Think on it. You look as if you could use a rest."

"Tessa, too?"

Slocum did not answer, and finished his steak in silence. It sat heavy in his belly, but it was a welcome feeling. Not often enough in the past few days had he had enough to eat.

"Should I come by the church later to help?" Slocum asked.

"No need. Things are quiet at the moment."

Slocum thanked Preacher Dan again for the breakfast, saw how the waiter watched him coldly, then left. If he could not persuade the father, then he would try the daughter. He went down the street to the hotel in time to see Tessa inside arguing with the clerk. Slipping in, he eavesdropped. She wanted an extension on paying their bill and the room clerk insisted on at least a token payment. It appeared that the Whitmores, for all their fund-raising, were running up bills they could not pay.

"In a few days. I can pay you then," Tessa said.

"One more night or I throw you into the street," the clerk said. Then he leaned closer. Slocum could not hear what he said to Tessa, but the intent was clear. She could work off her hotel bill by spending the night in the clerk's bed.

Her reaction was not what Slocum expected from a preacher's daughter. If she had slapped him or told him how insulted she was, that would have been normal. As it was, she only smiled and shook her head. Lifting her skirts, she spun and saw Slocum for the first time.

"Why, hello, uh, Jethro," she said loudly. "I see you've come to escort me."

Slocum glared at the clerk, who cowered back behind his counter. Extending his arm for her, Slocum led Tessa outside. The sun was barely above the mountain and already it was getting hot.

"Looks as if I came along at the right time."

"You are such a gentleman to escort me like this," Tessa said. "He was being awful to me."

"Sounds as if everyone in town is looking to get paid. You and your pa scraping the bottom of the money barrel?"

"Everything is going into the church. It is so costly, you know."

"You said you had a sizable poke in the bank. Thompson also said you could have a loan if you needed it. Why not take his money?"

"It is against our principles," Tessa said glibly. Slocum heard the lie in what she said.

"Get out of town," he urged. "I warned your pa, but he wouldn't listen."

"What? Before we get our congregation? The church must be finished. It is our duty!"

"There she is. Get her. Make her pay!"

Slocum looked past Tessa and saw four men come out of the general mercantile. The owner was sending his three helpers across the street to collect whatever Tessa and her pa owed.

"Stay back," Slocum said, putting himself between her and the men. "What can I do for you gents?"

"Outta the way, drifter," snarled the largest of the men. "The boss said she has to pay up or—" The man grabbed for Tessa. Slocum's punch traveled only a few inches, but connected squarely with the man's jaw. His head snapped back and his eyes turned glassy before he toppled to the ground.

"Who's next?" Slocum asked in a level voice. He didn't lift his fists. He stood with his stance wide and his hand resting at his right hip. From his relaxed stance, it was obvious to the other two men he could draw his Colt Navy from the holster and be firing before they had taken so much as a step toward Tessa Whitmore.

"Look, mister, Mr. Denbow told us to come over here. We don't want no trouble."

"Then help your friend back to the store. Mr. Denbow will get his money soon," Slocum said.

"How soon?"

Slocum glared at the slight man asking the question. Without another word, the two men grabbed their friend's arms and started dragging him back across the street.

"Things are heating up in Bitter Springs," Tessa said, "and I don't mean only the temperature."

"Let's go," Slocum said. Denbow yelled at his employees, berating them for cowardice. Slocum was tempted to go to the store owner and talk personally to him, but he suspected Denbow's courage extended only to employees he could browbeat.

"Not to the church. Somewhere else, please," Tessa said. She smiled her wicked smile and said, "The clerk wouldn't stop us going back to my hotel room. We could see how much we could get the temperature to rise in the room."

"Come on," Slocum said, taking her arm and steering her toward the church. She resisted for a moment, then gave in and accompanied him. Along the way, just in front of the café, they ran into her father.

"What's going on?" Preacher Dan asked. "You look so solemn, both of you."

Tessa tried to pass off the run-in with the store owner, but Slocum insisted on giving the preacher the full story.

"You need to pay some of your bills, or you'll end up making more enemies than converts," Slocum said.

"Gantt is behind this," Tessa said. "He has opposed us from the moment we said we were going to form a new church. Gantt does not like competition."

Slocum snorted. Competition between ministers for the souls of their flocks was hardly anything new, but he saw nothing of Gantt's hand in this.

"You didn't do a good enough job feeding rumors to the newspaper editor," Slocum said. Tessa looked surprised, but it was feigned.

"Come now, Slocum, let's not squabble among our-selves," said Preacher Dan.

"Doesn't look as if squabbling will be limited to just us," Slocum said. He pointed to a small mob moving down the middle of the street. "You have run up some big bills from the look of it."

"Papa," Tessa said, clutching her father's arm. "Maybe we should go, as John suggested."

"No."

Slocum was startled at the vehemence of the denial.

"You might end up at the end of a rope. That crowd doesn't look friendly."

"I'll fight for my church," Preacher Dan said. The deter-mination of only a few seconds earlier had changed subtly. Slocum tried to find the truth in what the preacher said, but couldn't. Then time ran out.

Denbow had found his courage, with a dozen men at his back. The small bulldog of a man shoved out his chin belligerently and shouted, "You pay up. Now. We want our money. You owe damn near everybody in this town."

"I don't owe any of the saloons," Dan Whitmore said softly. "Do you?"

Slocum wondered if he was intentionally angering the crowd. Without actually saying, he'd accused them all of being drunks who wasted their lives drinking bad whiskey.

"You pay up, preacher man!" The shout came from the back of the crowd, as it usually did. Slocum wondered if confronting Denbow alone would work, or if he needed to stop more than the store owner.

"Why don't you all write up invoices and give them to him?" Slocum stepped in front of Preacher Dan. If he could derail the crowd, he could get the Whitmores out of town. Then he could tell Rebel Jack he had found the can-non, and they could get on with their bank robbery. Right after he had found the two cannons, Slocum had worried about shots going astray and damaging not only Preacher Dan's church but the town. Now he was less concerned with what happened to the businesses in Bitter Springs.

"He knows what he owes. And we don't need to talk to you!" Denbow rushed forward. Slocum punched him, but the man fell forward onto him and knocked him to the ground. The rest of the crowd tromped over Slocum as they rushed to get to the minister.

Slocum rolled onto his belly and covered his head with his arms as he was repeatedly kicked. Then the crowd rushed down the street after Dan Whitmore. Finally able to force himself to his feet, Slocum ached in every muscle. Before, he had been peeved at the crowd and their way of letting one man think for all of them.

Now he was mad.

Slocum ran after the crowd just as Preacher Dan got up on a huge pile of dirt and tried to talk sense into them.

"Please, this is a house of God. Don't burn it down."

"Pay up, preacher man. You owe us!"

"You won't get the money by sinning," Whitmore said. To Slocum, this was as odd a note as accusing the men in the crowd of being drunks. Rather than slowing them, it gave impetus to their need to take revenge.

"Run him out of town on a rail! He's been spreadin' lies about Reverend Gantt!"

"Not him, his whore daughter! I seen the way she makes eyes at anything wearin' pants. She's the devil's daughter!"

"Don't burn my church. Please," Preacher Dan said.

This gave the notion life. Whether it was Denbow or another, Slocum could not tell, but someone lit a torch and ran toward the half-finished structure. Slocum drew and fired in one smooth motion. His bullet hit its target, though not exactly where he had intended. The man brandishing the torch let out a cry of pure pain and clutched at his right wrist. The torch fell harmlessly to the dirt.

"I been shot!"

"I was aiming for your head," Slocum said. He fired again as the crowd spun in his direction. "Get out of here. Mind your own business."

"He owes us! He owes us plenty!"

"Then make him pay. Don't burn down his church."

Slocum aimed his six-shooter directly at Denbow. The store owner got the message.

"We'll collect soon," Denbow said. "Come on, men. Let's get to plannin' on how to collect what's our due!"

The crowd followed its leader. Slocum slammed his six-gun back into his holster, then went to stamp out the torch. It sizzled and popped and filled the air with acrid smoke.

"How'd the torch happen to be so handy?" Slocum asked.

"You shouldn't have meddled," Tessa said, pushing him aside and throwing her arms around her father. The two of them left without another word. Slocum stared as they went, trying to figure out what was going on. If he hadn't known better, he would have thought the torch had been left there intentionally.

16

"You're lyin'," Rebel Jack Holtz said. He glared at Slocum. "What kind of deal are you tryin' to pull?"

"It's the truth," Slocum said. "I found the cannon. Fact is, I found two of them."

"Where? Not in that cesspit we were digging in," Holtz said.

"I went back to the mesa. That had to be the spot where the gun crew hid the cannon. Nothing else made sense. I dug a bit and found it—them."

"Two?"

"Two," Slocum agreed. "If we want to blow open the safe, we'd better get to work. There's a powerful lot that has to be done. I need gunpowder, wadding, a tamping rod, and most important, I need a few cannonballs."

"You didn't uncover any?"

"There might be some hidden, but I was all alone when I was digging."

"What size?"

"These were mountain howitzers with about four-and-a-half-inch bores. I seem to recall they fired twelve-pound balls."

"That's about the size of mine!" Rebel Jack laughed at his own joke as he grabbed his crotch and began dancing around.

For two cents, Slocum would have shot off Holtz's balls, but he needed the man's help getting the cannon aligned and ready to fire.

"Can you get the cannonballs?" Slocum asked. Holtz settled down and looked glum at this prospect.

"I was counting on finding the caissons. There's no trouble getting gunpowder. We're in the Guadalupe Mountains after all, and there's not a hill taller'n my head that's not been chewed on or blasted by some prospector. I can get the powder."

"The wadding and tamping rod are easy to come by. How many times do we have to fire the cannon?"

"That important?"

"It is," said Slocum, "if you intend to fire more than a couple times. I'll need a bucket of water to cool the barrel."

"Won't be necessary unless it takes you more than that to get the range."

"Howitzers were good up to nine hundred yards or thereabouts. All I need to do is calculate the proper elevation and drop the ball straight down on top of the safe."

"That shouldn't take but one or two shots," Holtz said optimistically. "Let's get our carcasses up to the mesa and do some more digging."

"I left the shovels there," Slocum said. "What about the cannonballs?"

"That's why we're going to dig up that entire damned mesa and make it look like prairie dogs have gone loco. No true Southerner would leave a cannon and not give us the shot to feed it."

Slocum wasn't so sure, but said nothing. Holtz rounded up the four men in his gang and they rode back through town. As they passed the church, Slocum saw no one working on it. If anything, it looked more like a mausoleum than a church. He hoped to catch sight of Tessa, but she and her pa were nowhere to be seen.

Slocum kept his head down as they rode south out of Bitter Springs. Only when he had passed the last building did he lift his head up.

"You get into some trouble in town, Slocum?"

"Jack, you've got no idea how happy I will be to see the last of Bitter Springs," Slocum answered. He led the way up the trail to the top of the mesa, and came out near the hole he had dug. He caught his breath when he thought somebody might have stolen the guns away. As he rode closer, he saw that the sides of the pit he had dug had crumbled, partially covering the howitzers again.

"Don't that about make the purtiest sight you ever laid eyes on?" Holtz jumped to the ground and slid into the hole. He brushed away the loose dirt with his hands. Slocum squinted as sunlight caught the bronze barrel.

"It's not made of iron," Holtz said, looking up. "Is that all right?"

"Better than all right. It's as fine as frog's fur," Slocum said. "Bronze doesn't rust."

"Then we're sure to have a pair of usable cannons!"

"Maybe not. Bronze does corrode. That would weaken the barrel. There might be other problems. These have been buried away in the desert for nigh on seventeen years."

"To hell with you," Holtz growled. "Everything's going to be just fine." He got his men digging until the air filled with sand and choking grit from around the two cannons. As they worked, Slocum took the opportunity to look for another spot where the caisson with the cannonballs might have been hidden. He doubted the soldiers doing the work of burying the cannon would want to go too far afield. Just west of the nexus on the rocky X, he found a likely spot and began digging. It took him only minutes to strike something hard and metallic.

"Found it," Slocum said. "I hope it's not another cannon. We've already got one more than we can use."

"Help Slocum dig," Holtz ordered. Slocum saw that the outlaw leader did very little of the hard work himself. If he provided the gunpowder, Slocum would forgive him for that.

Less than ten minutes later, they unearthed the caisson with four twelve-pound cannonballs packed away in a crate.

"We got the fixin's," Holtz gloated. "It's time to do some rollin' and then we can smoke!"

"We can get one of the cannons moved to the edge of the mesa," Slocum said. "That ought to give me a good idea of range."

As Holtz's men struggled to move the bronze cannon over to the edge, Slocum got an idea.

"I need to make sure the first shot or two is right on target. For that I need to mark the bank with a flag."

"Windage," Holtz said, nodding. "You get on down there and do what needs doing, Slocum. Me and the boys'll get the howitzer all set up."

"You have the powder?"

"Powder, balls, and wadding. We're all ready."

"The ram to get it all tamped in properly," Slocum said. "I'll get something when I'm in town. Put up a pole right in front of the cannon with a white cloth on it. I'll sight in on that when I get below."

"Don't just stand around jawing," Holtz said. "The sooner we get the cannon set up and firing, the sooner we will all be rich."

Slocum said nothing as he swung into the saddle and guided his mare back down to Bitter Springs. By now the horse knew the way, allowing Slocum to think hard without concentrating on the trail.

He took the back streets to avoid being seen by any of the crowd he had dispersed earlier, and dismounted behind the bank. Across the street he saw Preacher Dan's church, looking lonely and abandoned. Slocum pushed that from his mind. He had tried to help the Whitmores and had not gotten too far. Neither Dan nor Tessa had been the least bit appreciative when he had kept their creditors from setting fire to the church.

Slocum walked to the side of the building and looked up to the top of the mesa. A thin pole bent in the wind, a white cloth flapping wildly. He cursed. With such wind, even the short shot down to the bank would go astray unless he corrected exactly for it. He felt confident in his skills, but it had been a considerable number of years since his stint on the artillery battery.

He took off his bandanna and looked around for a pole to mark the range and give him an idea of windage. There were some across the street. Slocum hurried over and found one suitable to hold his bandanna, and another, thicker pole to use as a tamping rod on the cannon. He tied the bandanna at his head level, then worked to figure out where to stick the pole in the hard ground so it was on a line with the safe inside. He knew a few measurements would give him the best chance of sighting in on his target.

The bank would sustain incredible damage. A twelve-pound cannonball would blow the building apart—and anyone inside. Slocum wondered if he ought to fire one shot above the bank to scare patrons and tellers out. He didn't much care if Thompson stayed inside. He could imagine the banker throwing himself over the top of the safe to protect it with his own body.

Finding the right place, Slocum stuck the pole into the ground and made sure it wouldn't fall over. With this to use as a sighting device, he was sure he could drop the shot directly into the bank.

He stepped into the street and looked around. The cannonade would certainly send everyone in Bitter Springs scampering about like rats with their holes flooded. Then he looked at the church, and knew any mistake on his part would damage, if not destroy, the structure. Slocum walked to the shell of a church and looked around. Something struck him as wrong, but he could not put his finger on it. If Preacher Dan had built a berm against the tide of anger in the town, he could not have done a better job. The piles of dirt in front of the church were almost waist high and extended halfway around both sides.

Slocum called out to the preacher, but got no answer. For whatever reason, they had not parted on the best of terms, though Slocum had only tried to save the church from being burned down.

He kicked at some of the loose dirt and found another

torch. The rag at the end had been dipped in pitch and something that smelled like coal oil. A single match set to it would cause a blaze that could bring down half the town. Why Preacher Dan kept the torches around, so handy for angry mobs, was something Slocum did not want to think about. He picked up the torch and sent it spinning far off to land in the dust.

"Let them bring their own damned torches," he muttered.

Turning back, he took in the bank once more. This was likely the last time he would ever see it intact. Jumping into the saddle, he returned to the mesa carrying the thick wooden rod he intended to use as a tamping tool.

Slocum saw Holtz and his four men arguing bitterly near the cannon. From what he could see, they had done as good a job as possible setting the howitzer up, bracing it, and preparing it to fire. To one side, they had stacked the four cannonballs and some wadding. Beyond that, they had placed the gunpowder. It might not be a military crew working the cannon, but they had done a good enough job.

"What's wrong?" Slocum demanded.

"They say the gun's gonna blow up on 'em when they fire it."

"Why?" Slocum asked. One of the men pointed to a long crack down the side of the barrel.

"That's gonna split wide open if we fire it. I ain't standin' near the gun when it goes off."

"You might be right," Slocum said, running his calloused fingers over the crack. "Get the other cannon and—"

"There's no time," Holtz said. "We got to act now. *Now*, Slocum."

"Another hour or so's not going to matter," Slocum said, thinking it might give Thompson time to close the bank. It was better firing on the bank when the customers and employees had left. It would be dark then, but he could get the cannon aligned before the sun disappeared behind him.

"I want to take the other cannon down and use it on the

back of the safe if this doesn't work," Holtz said. "You fire, we use the other one close up."

"You remember what damage a cannonball can do," Slocum said. "You don't have to shoot at point-blank range to blow the hell out of a target."

"Fire this damned cannon. If that doesn't work, then we lug the other one down and shove it against the wall," Holtz said.

Slocum looked at the crack again.

"It might just be a deep scratch. I can't slide my fingernail in very deep," he said.

"See?" Holtz cried. "Do you see, you lily-livered cowards? You don't want to be rich. Well, I do. Let's fire this damned cannon!"

Slocum instructed the men how to load the cannon and ram in both gunpowder and wadding. He connected a lanyard and handed it to one of the outlaws. The man took it as if Slocum had handed him a rattlesnake.

"What do I do with this?"

"When I tell you, turn away and pull real hard," Slocum said.

"You ain't firin' it yerself?"

"I have to be sure it's lined up properly. That means I have to stand on the edge of the mesa. The cannon is set up a dozen feet back so nobody in town can see it."

"I don't want to fire it."

"Do it, damn you!" roared Holtz. "I swear, if you don't do as you're told, I'll kill you here and now." Holtz rested his hand on the stock of his scattergun. From the way his hand twitched, Slocum knew Rebel Jack would level it and fire at the slightest movement.

"Oh, all right. But I want an extra share fer this."

"Don't pull the lanyard till I give the signal," Slocum said.

"You ain't the boss."

"Pull it when *I* give the signal," Holtz said. "That all right with you?"

"Sure, yeah, fine," the man said sullenly.

Slocum and Holtz went to the edge of the mesa and looked down into Bitter Springs.

"I can see your bandanna flappin' around. That going to be good enough for you to get the range and windage?"

"I want to loft the cannonball over the church. It's a good thing they don't have a steeple on yet. Otherwise, we'd blow it clean off."

"The bank, Slocum, the bank. I don't give two hoots, a holler, and a good goddamn about that church. Can you hit the bank?"

Slocum said nothing as he lifted his field glasses and carefully watched the bandanna flutter about below. The breeze whipping down the main street was petering out. Moving the pole with the white flag on it around a little, Slocum got the trajectory worked out. With the two poles in a direct line with the barrel of the howitzer, all he needed to do was figure the arc the cannonball would follow.

"Hurry up, will ya? I'm gettin' antsy," the man holding the lanyard whined.

"We're almost ready," Slocum said. "The cannon is on target. I need to be sure it will arc up and come straight down on top of the bank. If I do that, the safe will be blown to hell and gone."

"Might be we should be ready to get into the bank as soon as possible," Holtz said.

Slocum could hardly believe the outlaw had overlooked such a detail. All the gang was up on the mesa.

"Do we fire?" Slocum asked.

"Hell, fire on the bank. It might take a couple shots to get everything right," Holtz said. "That will keep them scamperin' about like ants in a campfire."

Slocum stepped to the edge of the mesa again and watched the flag below. When it fell limp and unmoving, he would fire. He felt his heart hammering in his chest as he waited. He knew the men behind were equally as wound up.

"Get ready," Slocum shouted. The bandanna gave one last snap in the wind and then fell limply down along the pole.

"Fire!"

Slocum heard the man with the lanyard grunt with exertion as he pulled hard. The pin snapped out and the spark ignited gunpowder.

That was all Slocum remembered as the blast from the cannon lifted him into the air and threw him over the edge of the mesa.

17

John Slocum had no idea where he was. He floated, he drifted, he fell. It took a supreme act of courage for him to open his eyes, and when he did he still was lost. His head hurt like a son of a bitch, but that was a good thing. Dead men didn't hurt. At least he did not think so, and he had been close to death several times. When he had been shot in the gut by Bloody Bill Anderson, the pain had been excruciating at first. Then there had been a curious warmth and muzziness that enfolded his senses.

Not now. He hurt. He hurt bad.

As he reached out, his fingers brushed against something smooth before finding the sharpness of a needle. He yelped, but his voice was distant and muffled. Then he drew his injured hand in to him so he could stroke his own face. The bloody trail left behind brought more coherence to his thoughts.

When he focused his eyes, he looked down the sheer face of the mesa all the way to Bitter Springs. Slocum held back the panic. Whatever had happened, he was in no danger of falling. Slowly, painfully, he examined himself. His finger had touched the spine of a prickly pear cactus growing on the ledge just below the mesa top. It took a few more seconds for Slocum to figure out he was lying on the same ledge where the cactus had scrabbled out its precarious hold on life.

Groaning, he pulled himself up. His feet dangled over the ledge, causing another flare of panic. He quelled it. Then Slocum began pressing his fingers into his body. Plenty of scratches and cuts marred his skin but nothing serious. Standing, he peered up at the edge of the mesa.

"Holtz!" Slocum yelled again for the outlaw leader. No reply. Cursing Holtz and everyone in his gang, Slocum worked his way along the ledge, transferring to a higher one and then one still farther up on the face of the cliff. He finally tumbled out onto the mesa and sat up.

He thought he was in a bad way. Slocum quickly corrected that. The man who had pulled the lanyard was cut in half. The bronze cannon barrel had split and blasted forth a huge sliver of metal that had cut through the man like a scythe cutting winter wheat. Another of the gang sat in the dirt a few yards away, his head in his cupped hands. From the amount of blood, Slocum knew he had a head wound.

Slocum tried to stand, and his legs denied him. Crawling to the bleeding man, Slocum took off the already bloody kerchief and pressed it into the cut.

"You'll be all right. Press hard on your bandanna."

"It cut Rollins in two," the man groaned. "Just like that, he was flyin' all over the place."

Slocum tried to stand again, and found his strength had returned. A little. Holtz and the other two survivors in the gang were just standing, saying nothing, staring at the body of the artillerist. Slocum had seen plenty of men in shock during the war. All three of them would come to their senses in a while—or they would never be right in the head again. What mattered most to him right now was that he was still in one piece.

"Jack," he said. Slocum shook the outlaw hard and got his attention. "We should have used the other cannon."

"What do we do now, Slocum?"

"You can put the other cannon in place and we can try it,

but before we do that, I'd better get down into town and see
if the commotion was noticed." Slocum had no idea who
might have missed an explosion of this magnitude. Even
somebody passed out dead drunk would have been jolted
awake.

"Why not just go ahead?"

"It'll take you an hour to drag the second howitzer out
of the ground and get it into place." Slocum eyed the hole
in the mesa dug by the exploding cannon. That might have
been all to the good since the other cannon could be butted
up against the compacted dirt caused by the recoil when
the first howitzer barrel ruptured.

Slocum saw that Holtz wasn't thinking straight yet. He
left the outlaw leader and mounted his horse. The mare
shied and tried to buck him off. It took a few minutes to
gentle the horse and convince her he needed to return to
town. Once on the trail, the horse gave him no more problems, which was good since Slocum had a powerful lot of
thinking to do.

If he had an ounce of sense, he would reach the bottom
of the trail and keep riding. Anywhere. But the closer he
got to Bitter Springs, the more his nostrils flared. He swore
he could smell the gold in the bank safe. A lot of it. Enough
to make all his trouble worthwhile.

As he rode through the town, the reaction Rebel Jack
had predicted if their cannonball had landed was proving
true. The citizens ran around, shouting and crying, not certain what to do. But Slocum turned grim when he stopped
in front of Jensen's pharmacy. The old codger looked
downright smug.

"What's going on?" Slocum called.

"Don't know, but it ain't right. Sent my boy to Fort Suddereth to fetch the cavalry. Anything that causes that much
noise has got to be illegal."

"When?"

"Not a half hour back. Loud as thunder, it was. Ain't
heard the like since Sibley's detachment came through."
Jensen squinted at Slocum, then looked over at the brass

plate on the rock. "You wouldn't know nuthin' 'bout that, would you?"

"I meant, when did you send your hired man? Right after the blast?"

"The debris hadn't even stopped rainin' down when I sent him skedaddling to the fort."

Slocum looked around and saw bits of debris that had been blown off the top of the mesa. He turned grim when he recognized a severed human finger in the litter. Rollins had been cut in half and his pieces had been strewn all over Bitter Springs.

Without waiting to hear more from Jensen, he rode on to the bank. The debris had missed the bank building entirely. Some few bits of rock and dirt had fallen on the half-built church. Slocum wondered if Holtz might not have the right idea. Bring the other howitzer down, butt it up against the wall, and fire it point-blank. If it blew up, it would still destroy the wall and breach the safe. If it worked just fine, the result would be the same. The only problem Slocum saw with that was finding someone stupid enough to yank on the lanyard after Rollins had been killed.

He was about ready to return to the mesa when he took a deep whiff of smoke. The debris that had rained down on Bitter Springs had been a mixture of dirt, rock, human flesh, and fiery hot metal. He had no idea what had happened to the cannonball, but it did not seem to have left the barrel of the howitzer. He turned in the saddle.

His heart jumped into his throat.

"Fire!" Slocum jumped from horseback and hit the ground running. "Fire! The church is on fire!"

A piece of hot bronze must have landed in the middle of the construction. The fire lapped up at all four walls from inside. Slocum grabbed a bucket as he ran, dipped it into a watering trough, and, coming close to the front door before the heat forced him back, swung the bucket and sent the water flying. It turned into shining droplets in the air and immediately sizzled and hissed and disappeared in a cloud of steam. The fire had burned hot too fast for simple measures.

"Fire!"

This time, Thompson at the bank came out to see what the fuss was about. He bellowed out the same warning and in minutes, a dozen men ran to help Slocum. It did not matter what their beef with Preacher Dan Whitmore might be. If the church sent sparks into the air, the entire town would go up. The construction of Bitter Springs had been haphazard, and most of the buildings were like tinderboxes. The hot summer sun had added to the danger, turning everything bone dry.

"Form a bucket line," Slocum ordered. He was the only one who was keeping his head. The others milled about, mumbling, or tried to do ineffectual things alone. It took Slocum precious time to bark and snap and get the men working together, but he did.

"You have a volunteer fire department?" he asked the man next to him in the line.

"Nope, never had occasion. If a fire gets too out of hand, we just hitch up a team and pull the buildings out of the way."

Slocum had to admit this was an idea that had never occurred to him. But fire spread faster than horses could pull. The interior of the church was mostly empty, and that was all that saved Bitter Springs. The fire reduced the building to smoking embers, but they had prevented it from jumping to the bank and other nearby buildings.

"Get men onto the roofs and soak the shingles," Slocum said. "You, you, over there. You two, up on the top of the bank." Seeing an unexpected opportunity present itself, Slocum added, "I'll go with you. Bring buckets of water to put out any sparks or embers."

He jumped to the top of a rain barrel and then pulled himself up onto the bank roof. The two men he had ordered about as if they were green recruits reporting for army duty scurried around, sprinkling water on the few smoldering spots on the roof. Slocum walked around, gauging distances and seeing, now that the church was no longer an obstacle, how easy it would be to drop a cannonball straight down on the bank.

Going to the edge, he called down, "Hand me that pole with the bandanna waving on it."

One of the firemen tossed it up to Slocum, who caught it.

"What are you gonna do with that?" asked one man whose bucket was still half-filled.

"You never been in a fire, have you?" Slocum went around tapping the roof with the end of the pole. He figured where the safe would be, then drove the pole down into the roof so hard that it stuck upright. When he returned to the mesa, he would have an exact spot to aim at. Drop the cannonball here and the safe would be destroyed.

"Cain't say that I have. Still don't know what you're doin'."

"Marking weak spots," Slocum said. He had no idea what he would say if the man did not find this vague answer sufficient, but he did.

"Good," the man said. "Wondered if anybody would do that." He poked his friend in the ribs with an elbow and asked, "How come you didn't think of doin' that? Ole Man Thompson woulda skinned us alive if we hadn'ta found the weak spots."

"It's about time to belly up to the bar and have a drink," Slocum said. "Are you buying?" Seeing their hesitation, he laughed and slapped them on the shoulder. "That's all right. I'll buy. You two run along, and I'll be there in a couple minutes."

Congratulating themselves on a job well done, the two dropped to the ground and hurried off to the nearest saloon. Slocum had no intention of buying them drinks or even getting a shot of whiskey for himself. He had a cannon to fire and a bank to rob.

Slocum jumped down and went to get his horse. Before he mounted, he paused, thinking hard. He wanted to tell

Tessa to clear out. With the church burned to the ground, there wasn't much reason for her and her pa to stick around. Preacher Dan might want to rebuild, but it would be futile with no support in Bitter Springs for a new church. The way Tessa had gone after Reverend Gantt and how her father had left unpaid bills all over town had doomed any chance they might have had to make a home here.

The town was settling down, but Slocum felt as if a cocked six-shooter had been put to his head. Jensen had sent for the cavalry. How long it would take them to arrive was a question he did not want to stick around to answer. A day? Less, was Slocum's guess. But he had to see Tessa one last time.

He entered the hotel's side door and sneaked through the lobby. The clerk was dozing at the desk, snoring and then half-waking himself up so he could go back to sleep. He seemed to have missed all the excitement that had gone on through the afternoon.

Slocum went up the stairs and paused in front of Tessa's door. Just as he started to knock, the door opened. Surprise flared on her face.

"John! I didn't expect—"

He pushed her back into the room and closed the door behind them. On the floor by the door was her valise.

"You're leaving Bitter Springs?"

"I, uh, yes, Papa decided that it was for the best. He has the wagon about loaded and we're moving on. El Paso, I think, though he did not say."

"Good," Slocum said. "You know your church was burned to the ground?"

She nodded sadly.

"The mob did it," she said. "Papa would not give in to such things, but having so many of the city fathers against us . . ." She sniffed dramatically. "Well, it's for the best."

"Then I won't have to argue with you about leaving," Slocum said.

"You're leaving, too, aren't you, John?"

"I've got some business to tend to, then I'm going," he agreed.

"Am I that business?" She looked up into his eyes. He tried to read her expression and could not. Then he kissed her. It surprised her and she resisted for a moment, then responded.

"Oh, John, I wish you could come with us. But you have a different trail to follow."

Slocum found a different trail to follow. His hands slid down the woman's sides, down her hips and upper thighs, then went lower before coming back up. He felt the warmth of her bare legs as he hiked her skirt. His hands slipped from the insides of her thighs around to cup her buttocks. He squeezed down and then pressed forward. Tessa took a small step back, and then Slocum bore her down to the bed.

"Oh, John, hurry. We have to leave soon. Hurry. I want it fast! But I *do* want it!"

He silenced her with kisses, then lifted her a little off the bed so he could get her skirt out of the way. He pressed his fingers into the moistness welling up from between her legs. His fingers stroked across her nether lips until she trembled. He felt the pressure mounting within his own loins. It would have been good to make this last, to take the rest of the day with Tessa, but she was right. They both had to go.

Her hands fumbled at his fly. He helped her get his erection free. She took it in hand and urgently pulled him toward the tangled nest between her legs.

The tip of his shaft bumped into her and ran the length of her erotic valley. She moaned and lifted her legs. He repositioned himself and then stroked hard into her. They both cried out as he fully entered her tightness.

He looked down into her face. Sheer desire etched her every feature. Her eyes were closed and her lips parted slightly as her tongue peeked out. He slowly retreated until only the knobby end of his length remained within her. The sight of her breasts rising and falling under her blouse, the lust on her face, the heat and tightness, all spurred Slocum on. He rammed back into her and was rewarded with another gasp of desire.

She tensed all around him, squeezing down on his hidden length with powerful muscles. He thought of being crushed, and it was delightful. But he pulled back and then stroked forward faster now.

"Give me more, John. Hard. Fast. I need it so!"

He began thrusting harder, faster, then began moving in a small circle as if he was a spoon stirring around in a mixing bowl. The heat mounted and Slocum was lost in a tumble of emotions and sensations that finally caused him to spill his seed.

Tessa lifted her knees up to her chest and thrust upward to meet his every inward stroke. She cried out just as he got off. And then she sank down. Her hands roved easily over his arms and shoulders and finally his cheek.

"You are so wonderful, John. I wish things could be different."

"Things were mighty good, if rushed," Slocum said.

Tessa laughed easily.

"You have such a dry sense of humor." She pushed her skirts down and stood. "My, I will be walking bowlegged the rest of the day." She grinned at him. "I wish it could be that way tomorrow and tomorrow and tomorrow, too."

"You'd better hurry out of town," Slocum said.

"Is there something wrong?"

"Jensen sent for the cavalry after the explosion earlier."

"The cavalry?" She looked upset, then her cheery smile replaced the frown. "I'm sure they will be welcome in town."

"I'll carry your bag for you," Slocum said.

"Let's go out the back way. Papa said he would bring the wagon around in the alley behind the hotel."

Slocum didn't ask why. The people in Bitter Springs were not inclined to allow the preacher to leave without paying his bills, although Slocum counted the burned church as payment for about everything Preacher Dan bought.

He stopped at the back door and said, "The wood."

"What's that, John?"

"All the four-by-fours and planks were gone."

"I don't know what you mean. Oh, there's Papa now. Good-bye, John. Watch your back." Tessa stood on tiptoe and kissed him quickly but well, then took her valise and ran to the wagon. She tossed the case in and jumped up. She sat and waved to Slocum.

He thought there was just a trace of regret; then Preacher Dan got the horse pulling and the wagon rolled out. Slocum watched them leave. Something seemed wrong with the wagon. Then he pushed the thought from his mind.

He had a bank to rob and little time to do it before the cavalry arrived from Fort Suddereth.

18

Slocum paused on the trail up to the top of the mesa to watch Preacher Dan's wagon lumbering along the road toward the north. He waited until the wagon turned on a road going due west. Slocum knew he could get to the top of the mesa and ride down the broad slope westward and overtake them within the hour. He wanted to, but he wanted the gold in the bank more.

"Giddyap," he said, snapping the reins to get his mare moving. The horse obeyed, carrying Slocum one step at a time farther from Tessa Whitmore and her father. When he reached the top of the summit, he saw that Holtz had dragged the second cannon from the ground and had it in place. The pole with the white cloth fluttering on it was once more on the edge of the mesa, providing a convenient aiming device.

Rebel Jack and his three remaining men gathered about the howitzer, arguing. Slocum heaved a sigh. That was all Holtz and his gang did. For every crime they had committed, they must have argued over it for a week.

"Slocum, get your ass over here and aim the cannon."

"Good to see you've been working, Jack," Slocum said as he dismounted. He didn't like the man's attitude, although he understood it. He went to the cannon and looked at it. There was a deep dent in the bronze side. Dropping to his knees, Slocum put his hand against the metal. It was warm to the touch after being in the sun most of the afternoon, but the depression in the barrel was what caused him some concern.

"What's wrong, Slocum? I want to get on with this robbery. We already lost Rollins."

"We got more problems than that," Slocum said. "The pharmacist sent word to Fort Suddereth that there was an explosion up here. I don't know how seriously they'll take it, but they might send a squad out to investigate. The Apaches have been raising such a ruckus, they might figure it is part of a new attack."

Slocum stroked over the metal and saw that the dent went deeper than he had thought at first. No cracks. Nothing to show the metal had been ruined. But the dent was worrisome.

"Then quit your lollygagging and tell us how to point this damn thing."

"The barrel's got a dent in it. There might be another explosion if we use it."

Holtz grabbed Slocum by the arm and jerked him away from the cannon. Slocum spun and squared off, his hand ready to reach for his six-shooter.

"Look, Slocum, don't you go sayin' a thing like that. I *want* that gold. You line up the cannon and let me worry about everything else."

Slocum considered throwing down on Holtz then and there. The outlaw's attitude galled him.

"Don't touch me again, Holtz," he said. "If you do, one of us is going to end up dead. And it's not going to be me."

"You son of a—" Holtz stepped back, ready to go for the sawed-off shotgun dangling at his right side.

"Hey, boss, we're all loaded and ready," called the man holding the cannon lanyard. "When do I yank on this here string?"

"What's it going to be, Holtz?" Slocum had reached the point where he did not care. If he had to kill Holtz, fine.

Stealing the gold was important, but he had reached the end of his rope with the outlaw. He could go rob the bank by himself, if it came to that. Even if it meant he had to leave Holtz and his men with bullets in them.

Holtz's lips curled into a sneer, and Slocum saw the mad-dog killer he remembered from the war. The tenseness in Holtz's shoulders faded, though, and he backed away.

"The gold. I want the gold."

Slocum said nothing as Holtz spun and went back to the cannon to be sure everything was ready to fire. Turning his back on Holtz was not something Slocum cottoned much to, but he went to the edge of the mesa. He saw the point where he had been blown over the side and moved from it. If he had to die, let it be in a new spot.

The flag he had placed on the roof of the bank flopped about fitfully in the breeze blowing down the main street of Bitter Springs. Slocum moved the pole on the mesa around until it lined up with the target down below. He could not help noticing the burned-out husk of Preacher Dan's church.

And the dirt all around it. The piles looked even larger from above than they had from the street. The wall in front of the church had been extended around to the sides, as if Whitmore had wanted a rampart to hide behind.

"What's it going to be, Slocum? You intendin' to give the order to fire anytime today?"

"Hold your horses, Jack," Slocum called. He forced himself to look away from the ruined church to the flagpole. Adjusting the pole on the mesa one last time, he walked to the cannon and adjusted it. The line of fire was exact. He needed to guess how to lob the cannonball up in an arc that would come straight down into the safe. Marking the point with the pole below gave him a considerable advantage even artillerists in the war had not enjoyed. He knew the range, he had marked the target, he was shooting from a height, and—would the howitzer blow up like the first one had? He eyed the dent in the side and shook his head. There was no way to tell if an old cannon buried for so long would be safe.

"All ready," Slocum called. "Fire when you want."

The words were hardly out of his mouth when the lanyard was pulled and the cannon roared. Slocum saw it buck up into the air and back against the dirt cavity where they had braced it. The barrel flopped down and rolled a little. It had not blown up.

He ran to the edge of the mesa and used his field glasses to study the scene below. Dust had billowed up, obscuring the entire town. As it settled, Slocum let out a whoop. More by luck than skill, the cannonball had landed directly where he had aimed. There would be no need to use the other two cannonballs and risk the cannon barrel rupturing.

Slocum turned to congratulate Rebel Jack. He was alone on the mesa. Holtz and his three henchmen had fired the cannon and immediately ridden off. Slocum wondered why he had not heard them, then realized he was still deafened from the cannon firing. A tiny buzzing sound proved distant but growing louder, telling him he was regaining his hearing slowly.

"You son of a bitch," Slocum said. He turned and used his field glasses. More dust had settled and he saw the roof of the bank had fallen in. When he looked down the street to see the reaction of the townspeople, it was much as Slocum had expected. They milled about, formed tight knots, and pointed in all directions.

He lifted his glasses to the far northern end of the road coming down from the Guadalupe Mountains, and saw nothing. However, in the distance to the south, coming from the direction of Fort Suddereth, moved a dust cloud that could easily hide a company of cavalry.

Slocum started to run to his horse and go down the trail to warn Holtz, then stopped. If it meant his life—or his freedom—he was not about to dip his beak in that golden trough.

Thinking on it, he saw a way to remain safe and still get the gold—maybe. If Holtz got the gold loaded and came back, Slocum would share. That was such a slim possibility that Slocum watched carefully to see where the outlaw gang would ride. Tracking them would be easy enough, and he could collect his shares—and theirs—later. He still worried that Holtz would never get out of the town, with or without the gold, because of the riders coming so fast from the south.

Slocum decided his best choice was to simply do nothing but watch and see how the hand was played out. He waited until Holtz and his gang galloped through town, scattering men left and right. Slocum was not sure, but thought he heard tiny pops as the outlaws fired as they rode. It was no different from the days riding with Quantrill. Sporting as many as ten pistols so they would not have to reload, they always hurrahed a town, firing at anything that moved. Several hundred bullets could be loosed in the span of a minute, and then they were gone. Now Rebel Jack was using the same terrifying tactic to clear the streets of anyone who might get in his way.

Sucking in his breath, Slocum watched as Holtz and the other three owlhoots with him entered the bank. He waited. Nothing. Shifting his field glasses to the south of town, he estimated the soldiers were less than fifteen minutes away. They might have heard the roar as the cannonball crashed into the bank, and this had given them incentive to gallop into Bitter Springs.

The soldiers' horses would be all tuckered out. Slocum allowed as to how Holtz might escape since his gang's horses were rested. But it would be cutting it close.

"You got it, you got the gold," Slocum shouted. Holtz and his three partners ran from the bank and mounted. "Go north. Get out of town. I can track you till hell won't have it there. Don't get your asses caught by the army!" Slocum was not sure why he was cheering Holtz on like this since he was sure Holtz intended to cheat him out of his share of the gold. It might have been as simple as wanting the robbery to succeed because of the sheer audacity and the obstacles they had overcome to get to this point.

"You fool," Slocum said, following Holtz as he retraced his path, going south. Holtz would ride straight into the army's carbines and probably die. Holtz didn't have the good sense to slow his breakneck pace, ride along, tip his hat to the sergeant at the head of the column, and keep on riding. When he saw the soldiers, he would open fire.

Then all hell would break loose.

The riders vanished and the dust cloud south on the road neared at a slower pace now. Slocum reckoned those horses were tiring fast. He shook his head in dismay. Holtz could have escaped. And when he had, Slocum would have known the direction he had gone and could have tracked him down and gotten his share of the gold—and maybe a tad more for his trouble. Being double-crossed by Rebel Jack Holtz was not unexpected, but it wouldn't have gone unpunished.

Slocum felt the hoofbeats on the mesa before actually hearing the horses as they struggled back to the top. His hand went for his gun, then he relaxed. Holtz was flushed and so angry he was spitting without words coming out.

"What went wrong?" Slocum asked. The expressions on the other men's faces told the story as well as Holtz could.

"There wasn't any gold in the safe!"

"You mean the cannonball blew the gold up," Slocum said. He had expected any scrip to be burned, but gold coins were not easily destroyed.

"There's no damned gold in that bank! The safe was empty, 'cept for a pile of worthless papers."

"Deeds and shit like that," said one of Holtz's henchmen. "What do we want deeds for when you can't spend 'em on whores and likker?"

"We saw the soldiers unloading cases of gold. There should have been thousands of dollars' worth," Slocum said. There was no way Holtz and his men could be lying to him. He had watched them leave the bank. Why would they bother hiding their loot on the way back up to the top of the mesa if they intended to double-cross him? Slocum knew they would have ridden out like the demons of hell were nipping at their heels if they had found the army payroll in the safe.

"They musta snuck it out when we weren't looking," Holtz said.

Slocum did not think that was possible. He would have noticed a heavy wagon with soldiers returning. The merchants in Bitter Springs would not have been so outraged when it looked like Preacher Dan was not going to pay them if they had plenty of army gold jingling in their pockets.

"It's got to be the banker," Slocum said. "He must have taken the gold."

"He's dead, Slocum. He was sittin' right next to the safe when your cannonball came crashin' through the roof. Blowed him to hell and gone."

"There's no way of telling where Thompson would have hidden it," Slocum said.

"I'm gonna destroy the town. I'm gonna blow it up," Holtz said.

"You've got bigger problems," Slocum said. He grabbed the reins of Holtz's horse and led the animal to the edge of the mesa so the rider had no choice but to do as Slocum ordered. "Look south. Along the road."

"All I see's a dust cloud." Holtz's voice trailed off, then he swore a blue streak. "They're comin' from Fort Suddereth. I'm not getting my gold, and they've sent a company of soldiers after me!"

"How many people in town saw you come up the trail to the mesa? Anybody?"

"Hell, could have been every last mother's son of them," Holtz said. He jumped off the horse and let it snort and paw and then trot off.

"The soldiers will come after you. If you hadn't shot up the town while you were riding in, they might not have connected you to what happened at the bank," Slocum said.

He stared down into Bitter Springs wondering what *had* happened at the bank. Thompson struck him as a cautious man—definitely belt and suspenders when it came to money. What had triggered his paranoia about the gold in his bank? This was not the first time he had stored so much of the precious yellow metal. If anything, it was routine. There was nothing to make Thompson suspicions.

But the gold was missing.

"You said the cannonball hit straight on the safe?"

"Couldn't have been a better shot," Holtz said. "Right through the roof, angled down and blew the top off the safe, and kept on going."

"Could the impact have blown the gold all over the bank?" Slocum had never seen such a thing, but he was grasping at straws. He was positive Thompson had not spirited the gold away all at once. Had the banker stolen it one bag of coins at a time?

"Nothing but blood and dust inside," Holtz assured him. "What was left of the insides, that is. Blew a huge hole in the floor under the safe."

"Damn," Slocum said. He lifted his field glasses and saw who was riding into town—and it was not a company from Fort Suddereth.

"I know. That's why I'm gonna punish them!"

"Holtz, the riders aren't soldiers. It's a whole damn company of Texas Rangers." They might be after Holtz, but they were definitely after *him* because he had shot Ranger Jeffers. He could have talked his way out of any charges the army threw his way. There would be no convincing the Rangers of anything short of them putting a noose around his neck and letting him swing.

"I hate them as much as I hate Bitter Springs!" Holtz pushed Slocum out of the way and barked orders to his men. They had wrestled the cannon back into the dirt pocket in the ground.

"What are you going to do?" Slocum asked. His gut turned into an icy fist when he saw Holtz preparing the cannon for another shot.

"I'm gonna send the lot of them to hell!"

"They don't know you're up here," Slocum said. "Get away. There'll be other banks, more gold, better chances to steal it."

He wondered why he was arguing with Rebel Jack. The man's eyes were glassy now, and all reason had fled. Slocum owed him nothing. They had ridden together for only a short time, and Holtz had never been a friend. If anything, he was the worst of those in the war and a type Slocum had come to despise.

"Is Slocum goin' ta sight in for us?" asked the man nervously fingering the lanyard. Holtz furiously rammed wadding in and then stood back as his henchman rolled the twelve-pound cannonball down the barrel.

"We're firing straight into the cliff on the other side of town," Holtz said. "You ready? Pull the damned string!"

Slocum turned his back and clapped his hands over his ears as the cannon roared. He felt the hot blast of superheated gases on his back. A quick glance over his shoulder assured him the dented cannon had not bent or otherwise destroyed itself. Then the ground shook and the sound of tearing rock filled the air.

The screech rose until it almost matched the noise of the cannon report. Slocum did not need his field glasses to see the upper portion of the eastern cliff above Bitter Springs tumbling downward. The dust obscured his view for a moment; then he knew Holtz's revenge was successful. Half of Bitter Springs lay crushed under the avalanche.

"The Rangers are at the edge of town," Slocum said. He licked his lips and then chewed on his lower lip, wondering what the lawmen would make of the town's sudden destruction. "They don't know what to make of it. They might think it happened naturally. Rock slides are common enough in these mountains."

"To hell with that. I'm gonna kill 'em all!"

Slocum swung about, thinking he should put a slug through Holtz to keep him from drawing the Rangers' attention. Then he decided against it. The men with him were equally crazed. They had one last cannonball to fire. Slocum stepped far away, circled, and got onto his horse. Heading back to Bitter Springs was out of the question.

He turned his horse's face down the steep western slope and began the long ride to El Paso—and away from Rebel Jack Holtz and his crazy ways.

He hardly flinched when the cannon roared again, but he did ride a mite faster.

19

Slocum wished he had ridden away from Bitter Springs better prepared for the trail. He hunted for water and found none. He skirted the dry lake, and finally discovered a watering hole with slightly alkaline water. Hesitant to drink of it, he knew he had no choice. His canteen was empty, and he had several hard days' ride ahead of him, no matter which direction he went. Worse, he worried that his horse would get sick and die from the alkaline water.

"Just a drop or two," Slocum cautioned, but it was all he could do to keep the mare from thrusting her nose down into the water and drinking until she bloated. After a minute or two, he pulled the horse back. The touch of alkali did not affect the horse any, as far as he could see, but Slocum knew such things might take a while.

He filled his canteen and satisfied himself with thrusting his head into the water. He wished he had a bandanna, but he had left that back in Bitter Springs. After his all-too-accurate shot, both the bank roof and safe, along with his bandanna, had been blown to hell.

This got him to thinking. Holtz would never have tried lying about the gold being gone. Slocum knew Rebel Jack too well to believe he would run a bluff. If he had the gold and could get away with it, he would have shot his three partners as soon as the gold was stashed in saddlebags. Returning to shoot the cannon twice more into the town was an act of crazy vengeance and a way to work off his incredible anger at the robbery going bad.

"Thompson, you were quite a banker," Slocum decided. The actual way the banker must have carried off the gold coin was something of a poser, but he was the only one with a combination to the safe. Slocum wondered if the banker might have gotten wind of Holtz planning to rob the bank. It wasn't as if Rebel Jack or any of his men were tight-mouthed when they got drunk. More than once, the entire gang had sampled the pleasures offered by the Bitter Springs saloons. For all Slocum knew, they had sampled pleasures of the flesh, too. A soiled dove might have sweet nothings whispered in her ear, including boasts about how her paramour of the minute was going to be fabulously rich soon. A drunk man with a willing woman beside him might spill his guts about robbing the bank.

If a particular friend of Thompson was the one hearing this, she could have told him to get the gold out of his safe. Slocum stretched in the sun, squinted at the sky, and figured he had another hour or two of riding ahead before he camped for the night. He would have been a whole lot more content if he shared his bedroll with some of that gold.

"Come on," Slocum said, tugging on the horse's reins. "I want to put some more miles between us and Bitter Springs before we rest."

He had ridden all night and most of the next day without seeing any trace of pursuit. Still, Slocum was edgy about what had happened in Bitter Springs. If Holtz had succeeded in blowing up a goodly number of the Texas Rangers, the survivors would never stop until they had the culprit in their sights. Holtz would fight like a mad dog, but if they captured him, he would try to put the blame anywhere he could.

John Slocum was an easy name to give. There was no honor among thieves—or former army comrades.

He cut across barren land baked by the sun and sending

up shimmering heat waves that cooked him. When his mare began to stumble, Slocum knew it was time to go to earth and rest. He found a deep arroyo and got down the crumbling bank. The shade offered by the westernmost side was little enough, but a mesquite tree cast a long enough shadow for the horse. Slocum settled down, his back to the side of the arroyo, and fell into a fitful sleep.

Sometime after dark, possibly near midnight from the look of the constellations in the cloudless night sky, he heard creaking and clanking of wheels near enough to wake him. Slocum got to his feet.

"We might be in luck," he said, patting the patient mare's neck. "That just might be a Butterfield stagecoach on its way over to Hueco Tanks. I can ride inside and you can trot along behind without my weight tiring you out."

The mare only stared at him, one large brown eye unwinking.

"So, be a skeptic," he said, scrambling up the bank and walking a dozen yards. He had missed the road entirely in his wandering through the desert. The tracks were distinct. Twin ruts had been cut down into the dry ground some time back, and maintained by regular traffic that prevented the restless wind from covering it with sand.

Slocum dropped to his knees and examined the ground. The dim starlight provided all the illumination, but he let out a snort of disgust.

"Not a stagecoach," he decided. "The wheel marks're too narrow. And one of them wobbles something fierce."

Then Slocum brightened. The wagon that had passed by only minutes earlier was going west. The only ones likely to be out on the dry lake bed going in that direction were Preacher Dan and his lovely daughter.

Slocum returned to the arroyo, saddled his mare, and rode slowly along the road. In less than five minutes, he topped a rise and saw the familiar wagon rattling down the far side of the hill.

When he came even with the wagon, he found himself looking down the barrel of a sawed-off shotgun.

"What kind of reception is that for your handyman?" Slocum asked.

He did not hear what Preacher Dan said to Tessa, but she balked. She turned and argued with him a few seconds, then lowered the scattergun.

"You startled me, John. I wasn't expecting to see you again."

"Things heated up in Bitter Springs. I left in a hurry."

"What things?" Preacher Dan leaned over and fixed Slocum with a cold stare.

"Seems somebody robbed the bank."

"No!" Tessa exclaimed. She put a hand to her mouth in shock. "What's been done about it?"

"Not much. Rebel Jack Holtz dropped a cannonball smack on the bank and blew the safe apart."

"So this Rebel Jack robbed the bank?" Preacher Dan pulled back hard on the reins and lashed them around the brake. "Have the authorities caught him?"

"Seems likely they have—or have killed him by now," Slocum said. He described the carnage after Holtz had fired the cannonball into the far cliff and crushed half the town under an avalanche. "Don't rightly know how many Texas Rangers he killed either. He only had one cannonball left. Might have been effective. Even if he wasn't, they would swarm after him because he could never have killed them all."

"You seem to know a great deal about what went on, John." Tessa looked at him with the same steely look her father used.

"I was on the mesa watching it all."

"You helped this Rebel Jack Holtz person? You tried to rob the bank?"

"That about sums it up," Slocum said.

"You are a far more dangerous man than I realized," Preacher Dan said.

"Hope that doesn't stop you from letting me ride along with you. Where are you heading?"

"El Paso," Tessa said, though her pa tried to hush her.

"Oh, Papa, he's not stupid. Where else would we be going out here in the middle of the alkali plain?"

"You might be a lightning rod for trouble," Preacher Dan said to Slocum.

"That shouldn't bother a real preacher, should it?"

"What are you saying?"

Slocum swung in the saddle, hand going to his six-shooter. He did not draw.

"We've got a problem. A single rider's coming up fast. It's likely to be a Ranger."

Tessa moved the shotgun so it was hidden by her skirts, and her pa shifted in the hard seat, as if reaching for a six-shooter hidden at his feet.

"He's not likely to be alone," Slocum warned. "An entire company rode into Bitter Springs. Even if Holtz killed most of them, there might be half a dozen left."

"Hello!" came the greeting. "Texas Rangers." The lawman rode up. Slocum saw three more dark shapes appear out of the desert flanking him.

"Evening," Preacher Dan greeted. "What can we do for you? You look mighty parched. We got plenty of water, if you want to sample some."

"Doubt you'd have any firewater," the Ranger said, grinning. He had read the painted sign on the side of the wagon.

"Demon Rum," Preacher Dan said piously, "will send a man straight to hell."

"Expected you to say that. My pa was a minister down in New Braunfels. Never could understand why I preferred a nip or two instead of the sacramental wine."

All the time the Ranger was exchanging pleasantries, he was taking in details of Slocum—and Tessa. Slocum had to appreciate how she subtly moved about, causing the top couple buttons of her blouse to pop open and show generous swells of her breasts. No man, not even a Texas Ranger hunting for a suspect, would pay a whole lot of attention to anything else.

"Whatcha found?" came the loud question from one rider who had remained at a distance.

"A preacher and his . . . daughter," the Ranger said, grinning. "And what are you?"

"He's my hired hand," Preacher Dan said quickly. "Jethro tends the horses, does some carpentry work when we get to a town so I don't have to preach from the back of my wagon."

"He's so useful," Tessa said, turning so yet another button popped open. Slocum found himself staring more at her than the Rangers circling the wagon like vultures. He shook himself free of her undeniable spell.

As he did, his heart skipped a beat. Riding up was a familiar face. If it had been Ranger Jeffers, he would have gone for his six-shooter and tried to shoot his way free.

"You going to talk all night, Sergeant?" asked the young Ranger.

"Naw, we need to push on." The Ranger who had done most of the talking tipped his hat to Tessa, then said, "Have a safe trip. There's a lot of dangerous men out on these here plains." With that he trotted off, the others going with him.

All but the young Ranger.

He rode closer and stopped, staring straight at Slocum.

"You didn't have to let me go," the Ranger said.

"Nope."

"Thank you for not shooting me. I gotta admit, when I heard the shot, I thought you wanted to shoot me in the back. Then I saw what went on. If you hadn't fired, Holtz would have come after me and I would be buzzard bait."

"That's about it," Slocum agreed. "What happened to Holtz?"

The young Ranger grinned crookedly. "Rebel Jack got himself killed, along with two or three others in his gang."

"All of them?" Slocum had to ask.

Ranger Heyward nodded, then said, "We're huntin' fer Apaches."

"What about Jeffers?"

"What about him?" Heyward laughed, but there was no humor in it. "You didn't kill him, thanks to his lucky stars

and both a badge and a big belt buckle. Heaven knows I've
wanted to shoot him often enough myself. He is one mean
bastard." Without another word, Heyward galloped after
the sergeant and the rest of the Rangers.

"You two know each other?" Tessa asked.

"We've met."

"Under what circumstances?"

"It'll be fine. They're not looking for you," Slocum said.

"No, that one—the sergeant—was looking *at* me."

"I meant," Slocum said, watching both father and
daughter closely, "they weren't looking for who really
robbed the Bitter Springs bank."

"Whatever are you implying, John?"

"I'm not implying anything. You've got the gold from
the bank in the back of the wagon."

"A hidden compartment actually," said Preacher Dan.
"It keeps things more peaceable that way."

"For casual searches. Tessa makes sure any search
never gets too thorough."

"Why, John, what an awful thing to say." She let yet another button pop open, giving him a view of most of her
breast and the dark nipple cresting it.

"You can ride with us to El Paso," Dan Whitmore said.
"We might need some help with the wagon."

"The rear wheel's wobbling a mite," Slocum said. "I can
fix that again, though getting the wagon jacked up might be
hard with so much gold weighing it down."

"You're a clever man, John. You'll figure out how to do
it."

"I know lots of ways of doing it," Slocum said, grinning
at Tessa. "For a cut of the gold, I can probably think of
ways of fixing the wheel, too."

"What? You didn't do a goddamn thing to . . ." Dan
Whitmore's words trailed off.

"Some preacher you are."

"I am when it's convenient. Other times, I'm a traveling
mortician."

"I can see that folks wouldn't poke around a mortuary

either, giving you plenty of time to tunnel into a bank, cut through the floor of a safe, and empty it."

"What gave it away, Slocum?"

"The short wood beams. The planks. You dug the tunnel and supported the boards with the four-by-fours. I reckon your tunnel was not much more than a couple feet high, so you had to work on your belly. That's hard going."

"I'm experienced enough," Whitmore said.

"I don't doubt it. Tessa has plenty of experience getting folks in town to run you out, too. That makes for quite a diversion."

"We were ready to go when the crowd came to burn the church. I was quite vexed with you, John, for stopping them."

"You set fire to it yourself?"

"I had to," Whitmore said. "You put the fear of God into the crowd so they'd never get around to it any time soon."

"The dirt," Tessa said suddenly. "The dirt also gave us away. Isn't that right, John?"

"It is. I couldn't figure why so much got piled up. It all makes sense now."

A silence fell between them. Then Tessa said, "Let's find a spot to camp for the night and let the Rangers put some miles between them and us."

"I hope you're not intending to put any distance between you and me," Slocum said softly. He wasn't sure if her pa heard or not. It did not matter. They were partners now.

"No distance at all is the way I like it," Tessa said.

John Slocum had to agree. The girl and the gold and what looked to be a free ride all the way to El Paso. What more could he ask?